It's My Life

It's My Life

Let Me Live the Way I Want

PRAJYOTI PATI

PARTRIDGE
A Penguin Random House Company

To order additional copies of this book, contact
Partridge India
000 800 10062 62
orders.india@partridgepublishing.com

www.partridgepublishing.com/india

Dedication

This book is dedicated to the only girl of my life, my Angel. Thank you, Angel, for making it possible for me.

"It's not for you to listen or read or understand or execute. Neither it is for you to pass time nor repent. It's for you to think beyond the thoughts, dream beyond the dreams and live as no one has ever lived. Live as you want, not as your parents or siblings or friends or relatives want. No one can fit into your shoes nor can you fit into anyone else's. No need to pacify, no need to justify, you know what you are and that's what matters at the end of the seconds. And yes, no need to second anyone. So many people tell you so many things, advise you so many things when neither you need something nor you expect. And the best part is the advisors, the well-wishers and the guides who forget all those beautiful suggestions when they get into the same pit. Does it sound funny? Oh! It really is not. It's hilarious. I laugh out loud when I think about these so-called two-legged creatures known as human beings. And no one but me enjoys the echo of my own devil's laugh. I am not lonely although I am alone. I don't let anyone pity my aloneness as they are too naïve to misunderstand it. I am beyond all these emotions. And I bestow my gratitude upon you for showing me the path to revive myself and leave the feelings behind. The closed doors are opened to visualize my soma in the mid of Antarctica and in the Sahara and in the Pacific." Said Sayuri without a pause.

Her breathless thoughts left him stunned. His eyes were wide open. His mind was disturbed as he has never heard her speaking in such glibness. He was astounded with her volubility. He has never seen her speaking with such depth. He thought whether it was the same tacit person with whom he had lived for half a decade or was she someone else. This part of her was never revealed to anyone at any point of her life but to her own self.

She went numb after speaking out so much with a wonder. She thought to herself "what made me share my thoughts with someone like him? Is he so important for me? Will he understand the meaning behind the words? Why didn't he interfere? What is going on in his mind now? Why am I uncontrollable? Am I in love with him?" Her inquisitiveness came to a pause when the smell of the lily intruded.

She touched his left cheek to break his numbness. He was so afraid to utter a single word. Rising from his senselessness, he wished to leave the garden and run away as far as he could from the shade of the tree. He wanted to run till the sea shore and swim till her fear released him. He was shivering inside and only she could feel his fear. Anyone else with him could never have known how afraid he was. She knew people around her so well that she did not need any clarification.

Fear? What is fear? What was he afraid of? Was he afraid of her? Why? Was it just because she had spoken so much? Or had she committed a crime as this is a male dominated society? He was unsure of everything. However, he was certain about his intuition that she was the one who could understand his silence, read his eyes, and feel his numbness. He had never felt this for anyone even after being with so many people. He was not a bisexual but he never had this feeling for them whom he refers as his best buddies.

The tree above shaded some of its flowers, the birds chirruped and the wind blew. She held his hands in hers, looked into his eyes and told him, "You do not need to be afraid of anything. Fear nothing but your own self. No one has the power to betray you, belittle you, demean you or demotivate you but your own self. No one cares about you or think of you but you. Then why and what are you afraid of? Fear is nothing but a thought generated in the mind because of some aberration or some unusual happening which kills all the positive feelings. Almost all creatures have phobias and the two legged creatures top the chart. So many of these creatures have the fear of so many things. I have seen some of them afraid of water, some are afraid of heights, some are afraid of darkness, some of them are afraid of commitments, some of them are afraid of emotions and feelings, some of them are afraid of truth, some of them are afraid of love, some of them are afraid of accepting their fault, some of them are afraid of the nature, some of them are afraid of other human beings and most of all they are afraid of dreaming. Why don't they release themselves from these fears? Why have they tied themselves with these shackles? Why don't they free themselves? And the irony is that these questions never mattered to me.", she inhales the smell of the white lily.

"Is not there anything in this world which they are not afraid of?" he asked with a quivering voice.

She looked directly into his eyes and with a silent smile; she replied "There are so many things which most of them are not afraid of. They are not afraid of hurting others, they are not afraid of digging pit for others, they are not afraid of taking others for granted, they are not afraid of giving advices and suggestions to others, they are not afraid of asking others to be like them, they are not afraid of spreading rumours out of nothing, they are not afraid of changing the character of a girl to a virago and a guy to a bastard, most of them are not even afraid of defending themselves if they are incorrect, they are not afraid of getting carried away, they are not afraid of getting mad for no reason."

His grey cells became over-active. He thought which category he fell into. He never had such a conversation ever in his life with anyone, not even with his own self. Until this moment, he always had a notion that he was mature enough to handle any situation. He understood this nature more than anyone as he understood the human beings and their feelings. He wondered about his thoughts and pondered about his perception about himself. He convinced himself that he couldn't be right. Somewhere something was wrong. He had never been told that he was wrong and was always appreciated by the people around. But today the golden words of his own wisdom compelled him to introspect. His introspection led him to blank eyes and a heavy mind.

His thoughts and her mind were intruded by their colleagues who walked towards them. While exchanging a "Hi", one of her colleagues asked," hey, what's goofin' up between you two?"

He replied," Nothing at all and I need to be excused now." with a sincerity.

"Thank you so much." he said to Sayuri while leaving.

"Why such arrogance? What attitude is this? What's wrong with him? Is he insane?" were put across by the uninvited colleagues.

"He might be disturbed or lost in thoughts. Besides, everyone is insane, including you and me. Only the degree of insanity varies." she replied with a smile.

"Why do you always back him up?", one of the colleagues asked.

"Never did. Never will. For anyone." she asserted.

"Then why did he thank you?"

"The answer also left with him. You are asking the wrong question to the wrong person. You could better have asked him."

"Hey buds, calm down. Don't het yourself up. She is so naïve. Stop pulling her.", interrupted the other colleague of theirs.

The smell of lily vanished with the smoke of cigarettes lit up by the guy. The girl took a puff and returned it to him. The smell irritated Sayuri as she was irritated by loud music, honks, raised voice and people who got into her nerves like these two collegaues. They always poked into her and were eager to know about her. She turned them down with a killer smile. They had decided to bug her every time they got a chance and she has decided to become oblivious to their comments.

She gave a smile and bid bye while leaving them.

"I do not understand her.", said the guy.

"Even I do not.", replied the girl while the smoke came out of her mouth.

She overheard them and gave a sarcastic smile to herself.

She was waiting for him in the evening at the bus stop as he always did. He never left without her and if he ever had to then she was well informed by him. They both worked in different MNCs next to each other and their relationship grew at this bus stop while waiting for the bus. She was always thankful to the Government for having this bus stop near to their offices for which she got a chance to meet him. She thanked herself a million times for having him in her life.

She was worried and irritated. She was worried as he always reached on time and informed her if he had to be late or he had to leave early. And she was irritated as she never liked to wait. If he had to stretch at office then she also said that she was stuck up with some assignments and she would be late so that she could leave with him. She never missed a chance to be with him.

But today, she was astounded with this aberration. She tried reaching his number but the number was switched off. She tried reaching his office number and after trying repeatedly she was told that he left office in the afternoon.

She was distraught and her eyes were filled with tears. Her emotions were shattered and she took an auto directly to his room. What happened to him? Is he alright? Why did not he tell me that he was leaving office? Is he angry with me? Did he meet with an accident? Oh God, No. Don't do that to him, keep him well. Nothing should hurt him ever. Dear God, please keep him in safe hands. She reached his room with all these thoughts.

She rang the doorbell repeatedly without any response. She knocked the door and the effort was in vain. She was devastated within and was about to ask his neighbour whether he had been to the room or not when the sound of the door knob relaxed her. He slightly opened the door to see the guest when she entered in to his room by pushing the door and slamming behind.

He was benumbed to see her as he had never invited her to his room and she had never been to his room. Before he could think of anything, she gave him a tight slap. He was taken aback with this act of her. He was drunk and his grey cells were either hyperactive to think anything or numb enough to react.

"What the hell is this? Why did not you tell me that you are not there? What's wrong with you? Why did you keep me waiting for so long? Do you like to stress me? Do you have any idea how stressed I was? Do you know what was going on within me? Do you have any God damn notion what I have been through in the last few hours? Can't I speak my mind out? Can't I be me with you? Don't I have the right to speak to you the way I speak to myself?" and she started crying.

She wrapped her arms around his neck, rested her head on his shoulders and cried. She cried out loud. He did not pacify her. He let her cry. He believed that the person who cried in front of you was the person who was most comfortable with you and trust you. Tears are the emotions which should never be hid just like the smile. Tears are part of an emotion which can never be shown in front of everyone like a smile or happiness or laughter, and when it's shown, it should not be stopped.

She stopped crying after a few minutes, released him from her arms and slapped his other cheek before settling down on the sofa.

"What?", he asked.

"Can't you ask for a glass water, duffer? I have come to your place for the first time."

He brought a glass of water with some mint flavour in it and handed over to her.

"I won't drink. You help me with that."

He helped her drink the water and kept the glass on the table and sat on the floor, looking at her.

"Why did you leave office in the afternoon and did not care to inform me?"

He came closer to her. He held her hands, looked straight into her eyes and confessed, "Je t'aime".

"What?", she exclaimed.

"I was informed that you have studied French. I guess I was misinformed."

"No, I know French. But are you serious?"

"What do you think?"

"No, are you really serious"?

'Do I look like I am kidding with you?

"No, but…"

"But what?" he interrupted, "I was never ever so serious about myself, forget about my god damn life."

"Since?"

"A long time. I do not remember since when."

"Why did not you ever say this before?"

"Because I was waiting for you to confess. Besides, you have always told me that your parents matter a lot to you. They have dreamt a lot and have a lot of expectations from you. They want someone from your caste who is highly educated and well-established. Your dad wants a guy from the same caste with a well-settled job who must be from a decent family and accept your parents like his. Your mom wants a guy who should be from your community, who is financially sound, should have cook and maids for the daily chores so that you won't have to do anything. She expects you to live your life like a Queen. Every mother wants her girl to live such a life. And I was afraid because I am not from your community. You are an East Indian and I am a West Indian. Our cultures are different, our style of living is different, our mother tongue is different, and our festivals are different. Your parents will never accept me and you care for them a lot. I don't think that you will ever leave them for me and I can never meet their expectations. I live my life in my own terms, I will definitely try to fulfil all your wishes, keep you as my Queen and not let you do the house hold chores and give my best to keep a smile on your face but what about your parents who need a guy from your caste or community? That's the thing which I can't take care of."

"Hey, sweets?"

"Hmm?"

"Don't worry about anything. I believe in you and trust you. I understand that my parents have so much expectation but I believe that we can make it. You just have to be strong enough and settled properly so that you can speak to my parents and I can expect a positive response. I will tell you when the time comes so that you can come and speak to my parents, Ok?'

"Okay."

"And yes, je t'aime aussi.", she whispered while planting a kiss on his cheek.

His feelings were ineffable and he wanted her to be with her the whole evening and night and forever. She turned to leave and hugged him tightly before leaving.

"Never dare to leave me." she ordered.

"Can I tell you something?"

"Hmm?"

"I love the way you say 'hmm'. Can I call you 'Saaya'?

"Why so?"

"You are my shadow. Shadows always stay with the light and I want light in my life, I need no darkness and you only can get light for me in my life. I want you to bring light in my life and stay with me as my shadow forever. I want to have a light of hope in my life and you should be there next to me as my Saaya."

"In a pensive mood, Dumbo?"

He smiled.

"Yes, you can. I would appreciate to be your shadow and remember you will get bored with me some day in your life and still I will not leave you. I will always stay with you as your shadow. No one can ever let this shadow go away from you, not even you."

"If I ever get bored with you then I will fight with you or do some mischief to bring some spice in life, and I hope you will never leave me because of the fights." he said with tearful eyes.

She hugged him tightly and planted a kiss on his left cheek.

"Why did you learn French?"

"I love France and want to visit that place at least once in my life. I would be the luckiest girl in this world if I could visit that place again and again, over and over. I am in so much love with that place."

"You can never love that place more than I love you. And yes, I will congratulate you for being the luckiest girl."

"What do you mean?", she inquired with a bewilderment

"Nothing. ", he avoided, "Why do you love that place so much?"

"People are so lively. They are so much into love. Even you can find best of the perfumes and leather bags. That place is the hub of fashion designers. And you know what?

"Ya?"

"Most of the happiest countries in the world lie in Europe. They live their life, they do not spend their lives, as you know the difference between living and spending, and they live every single second. They are least bothered about their job. They give time to their family, their hobbies, their professional life and whatever they want to give time to. We are just struggling to earn more, live a better life, maintain a status, own a bungalow, a car so that people can say that how rich he/she is."

"Don't you think that the happiness lies within the eternal self?"

"Yes, it does. However the external affairs matter a lot too. It matters when you get up in the morning with full of life and find that the water is not coming out of the tap because the society has announced yesterday that there won't be any water supply for two days, it screws your mind. When you switch on to press your clothes and find that there is no electricity, the mood is affected. When you come out of the house, an illiterate driver with mere common sense driving a luxurious car will spill water on the road because of the pits, the internal calmness vanishes. When you get inside the bus or train, you will see people fighting over some silly things or pushing you or stepping upon you without giving a damn to you, does matter to have an uncontrollable feeling. When you come out of the office in the evening and ask a cab or auto driver to help you reach your destination and most of them will turn you down, then the headache begins.", she exhaled "Happiness lies within, we have got all the guts to have control over our own self but how long or how much. We are human beings with so-called emotions and emotions do vary with circumstances at some point of time."

"Have you always been so logical?"

"I do not know, never wanted to know whether it's logic or a mere conclusion. I always want to have a satisfied answer for self. I do not want to take myself for granted by giving some mere excuses. If I cannot see the invisible things behind the visible then I am worthless being a human being. If I can't find the meaning within the words then I can never understand anyone. That's what I believe in."

"Well, let's go. Your parents must be worried. I will drop you at your place."

"No. It will be a problem if someone will see. I do not want anyone to know about us now. You are my precious. Don't worry, I will manage.'

"It's already late, I will drop you. I won't go till your home, I will get down before that. Fine?" he insisted.

"Alright."

They both stepped out of his room and he was about to lock the door when she asked him to open the door. He opened the door without asking her for the reason.

She entered her room and pulled him inside closing the door behind.

Before he could realise anything, she hugged him tightly and he felt her breathe. He went numb and started crying inside his heart.

"Shall we leave now or do you want to stay back?", he whispered.

She released him and went outside the room. While walking down the steps, she thanked him.

"For what?"

"For letting me be ME with you. I have never been so comfortable with anyone; I had never spoken my mind to anyone apart from myself. I am really happy that you let me do this and responded exactly the way I behaved with myself when I spoke to myself. Thank you for being so interested in me, in knowing me, in understanding me and in listening to me rather than hearing me."

"How many more times are you going to thank me?"

"Once more." she replied with a teasing smile.

He was looking out for an auto and every single auto was turning them down.

"Crap.", his frustration came out.

"See, this is what I was talking about then. Your happiness was taken over by irritation or as they say, frustration."

He looked at her, gave a smile and winked.

She crossed her fingers with his and rested her head on his shoulders while going back to her home.

They reached and before he could say anything, she put her finger on his lips not to utter a word. She wanted to feel the silence of his and understand his silence.

"Don't say anything or else I will come back with you to your room tonight."

"Then it will be our home, and there won't be anything like yours or mine. Everything will be ours."

"Sshhh…. Good night."

"Sweet night, Saaya."

He grabbed some chocolates, fried chicken and ice-cream while returning back to treat himself. He always did treat himself when something really great happened in his life or when he was extremely happy or at some special occasions like his birthday.

It was his special day. He could finally feel her presence in his life. Someone with whom he could settle down and have a happy life forever without feeling his own emotions all alone.

His phone beeped several times and he did not bother to get up and see whose messages were coming. He knew that the messages were coming from her but still he did not care.

After two hours, he grabbed his phone and saw the number of messages.

"Hey, Sweets, had dinner?"

"Where are you?"

"Are you there?"

"Did you sleep?"

Get up na, I want to listen to you for a few minutes and you sleep after that."

"You seriously slept. ☹ "

"Missing you, sweets. Good night."

He really felt sorry for not replying to her messages and was happy that he was about to give her a surprise.

"Sorry, Saaya. The phone was not with me and I was busy with something. I am really Sorry. I am missing you too. Do you want to know what I was busy with?"

"You are my light at night

You are my shade in the broad day light

I see not me but you in my shadow

Just like the sun rays enter through the window

They pray Him for every sadness or happiness
And I thank you for making my life a bed of roses
You are nothing but my guard
As you are there with me, I am never sad
I love the way you care
I too love the smell of your hair
Thank you for letting me be a part
And thank you for what you are."

———◆◈◆———

The sun was setting, the moon was rising, the birds were returning to their nest, mercury was falling when a soul entered into a body and came out from the darkness of the womb to the enlightened world with a scream which was followed by tears to let the people around know that she has arrived. Everyone around her was smiling, grinning and sharing their happiness. And she was the only one crying out loud till her mother took her in her arms to have a close look at her to feel how beautiful she was, how beautiful her eyes were. She was such an angel!

Her father was a government employee and her mother did all the household chores. She weighed less than the average weight of a new born baby and struggled to survive for first few days. Her dad was really happy to have her in his life and was terrified with her health. He was an atheist but went to the God's home for the first time in his life to ask for his daughter's recovery. He pleaded to the doctors, day in and day out, to save her daughter. He was poignant for the first time in his life.

He cried his heart out when the doctor said that she was perfectly fine and can be discharged from the ICU. He took a month's leave (paternal leave) from his office to take care of her. His ineffability crossed all the limits. His feelings were inexplicable.

His wife was beaten up whenever she fell sick.

"Why the hell don't you take care of her? Why is she falling sick so frequently? Do you want me to leave my job and stay home all day to look after her? I can very well do that as she is my daughter. Why don't you start looking out for a job if you can't look after my daughter?", he used to growl.

She remained silent. She never uttered a single word. She was an example of naiveté. She never hurt anyone either with her actions or words. She believed that the truth was triumph and devotion to family was devotion to God. She feared God. She never let anyone know about her own feelings or health. She always carried a smile on her face to hide all her pains and sufferings. Moreover, she loved her child, whom she gave birth after going through so much pain, more than her husband. She cried whenever her baby girl was going through any pain and she stayed beside her throughout the day.

Her father was a shrewd, irritating, short temper dipsomaniac. He was the best for everyone in his world. Whoever came across him once, praised him. He had the magic within himself to attract people and deal with them extraordinarily. Even his wife thought herself to be the luckiest woman to have such a husband in her life irrespective of how much she was physically tortured and mentally harassed by him. He treated her as her slave. He took all his frustrations out at her, shouted at her, and tortured her physically till she bled.

She had devoted herself completely to him. She believed him to be his eternal soul and she was nothing without him. She never protested. She never defended herself. She accepted everything which came in her way. She did her daily chores even when she had a temperature or a swollen leg or hand because of the physical torture. She loved her family and kept her family's sanctity all the time.

On the special naming ceremony occasion, he threw a grand party and invited every single person he knew to share his happiness. No one could believe the reason behind his happiness. People have girl child, although female foeticide happened, but what was so different for him on having a girl child? Most of them had a question mark on their face. They had this question not because of the baby girl, it was just because they were jealous of him, envious of his happiness.

He named her "Sayuri".

Everyone congratulated him for having such an uncommon beautiful name. He was sure that no one knew the meaning of that name and no one cared to ask him and everyone congratulated him as a sign of formality.

Guests came and left. Sayuri slept on her mom's lap. But his happiness remained intact.

———◆———

By the time she got her consciousness, she was blessed with her best friend, her brother. As the time passed, they got closer to each other, sharing everything with each other, fighting with each other, waiting for each other at dining table, cuddling each other, showing each other's love to each other. But the only responsibility which she took care from her early age was the dwelling mood of her best friend, her brother.

Her childhood was annihilated because of the gruesome fighting between her parents. Her mother never uttered a single word but her father abused her mother, slapped her, kicked her and shouted at her. He mostly did all these when he was drunk and when he was not drunk, he remained completely cold. He did not talk to her or allowed her to speak a word.

He never did anything in front of his children. He adored them a lot. Irrespective of how drunk he was, he always locked them in a room before doing all these. However it affected the two little kids a lot. Their cacophony took their sanity, her mother's weep made them lose their sleep. They could not concentrate on anything.

Once she managed to unlock the door and when she came out, she saw her father beating her mother ruthlessly with his leather belt. She was wailing in the corner of their bedroom and pleading him not to beat anymore. He instantly stopped beating her when he saw Sayuri in front of him. She was in a state of shock when she saw blood on her mother's body. She decided not to leave her alone from that day on and whenever her father came back from the office, she deliberately stayed in the room to protect her and never let her father lock her anymore.

Her father loved her so much that he started coming early without getting drunk and helped her with her studies. Her family started being better when the chaos deteriorated. She became close to her father and started gaining knowledge on various subjects and her respect for her mother increased day-by-day. The more she stayed with her father, the more she respected and loved her mother.

Her father was never had any inclination towards his son which repelled him from him. He got close to his mother and sister as he neither received love nor pamper nor help in studies from him. He deliberately secluded himself from his father even before he had got his consciousness. He was always taken care of by two beautiful ladies in his life, his mother and his sister. They never let him down anywhere.

He was always beaten up by his father because he always went against him and intentionally did things which he never liked or wanted. He sometimes refrained himself completely from his father and did not reply to him even after he asked him about his examination results a few times.

The two ladies in the family took care of the cold war between the father and the son. Mother-son, mother-daughter and brother-sister relationship were in full bloom. They played round the house, made drawings, taught each other, massaged each other and pampered each other when her father was not around. Sayuri, by all of them, and her brother, by her and her mother, were brought up as pampered children.

She excelled in all her examination, topped the oratory competition, topped the calligraphy competition, topped the singing competition, topped the debate competition, and topped the quiz competition and all other in-house competition. She excelled in her academic career dramatically by letting others far behind. She was never athletic, never participated in any sports.

Her friends envied her everywhere because of her excellence and her teachers were carried away by her wit and interest to learn things. Apart from her friends, everybody liked her because of her talent, communication, decency, attitude and her respect towards elders. She never missed a chance to show her gratitude towards her parents and family whenever she was praised in front of anyone.

On the annual day of her school, she always won the best student award apart from other awards. Whenever she was handed over the microphone, she would start with,

"I am really thankful to my Mom, my dad and my little naughty brother for letting me bag these awards. It's not the result of my efforts; it's the result of their love, support and care. Thank you Mom, dad and my sweet little innocent brother."

Her parents felt proud of her and every time she got some accolades, her dad boasted to everyone around about his daughter's achievement with a sense of pride and her mother treated her family with some special dishes.

The anger of her father had diminished, her mom was out of the turbulence and the father-son relationship was recovering although there was a glitch from her brother's side. He was unable to forgive his father and forget those dreadful screams of his mother. This always created a gap between him and his father. All the efforts made by his father to make the relationship stronger with his son went in vain. He never let him cross the line and always maintained a safe distance from him. He became famous among his friends because of his co-curricular activities and his knowledge in bikes and cars attracted the masculine group. He was average in his academics but brought laurel to his parents and school in sports. He respected and obeyed only his mother and fought only with Sayuri whom he called fondly as "Sayur". He behaved as if his father did not exist and bestowed all his love upon his mother and sister.

She was the apple of her parents and a genius at her school. With time she became a gorgeous girl with the most beautiful pair of eyes which said everything about her before she parted her lips. They say that the eyes are the door to the heart but her eyes were the road to her soul. She was incredibly beautiful, she possessed knowledge about mythology, science, sports, politics, history, economics current affairs, defence, movies, songs, and what not. Ask her anything and the answer was on the tip of her tongue. There was nothing she was unaware of. If she ever came across something which she was unaware of, she spent hours to know every single thing about the subject like what was that, where had it come from, what was its' current existence and whatever question came into her mind. Her inquisitiveness was insatiable. Her teachers were baffled at her and sometimes they were scared to face her as they did not have a satisfactory answer to her question. They appreciated her but could not feed her with enough facts.

She had nothing in her mind but her career and her family, rather her family and her career. Her mirthfulness invited all the positive energy to her. She had always been focused. If she needed something, she had always got it at any cost. When she was certain of something, she was bestowed upon with that. Either with her efforts or luck or parents benefaction, she had always received whatever she wanted.

The guys in her school started hitting on her and she never gave a damn to any of them nor bothered to speak to them. There was a fair-looking studious guy who had just stepped behind her, in every academic year or co-curricular activities and had feelings for her. However he never spoke to her. He stared at her, felt for her, dreamt of her but never had the guts to speak to her or exchange a "Hi" and she never bothered to know what was going on among her friends or classmates. She had only a few friends with whom she either had lunch, went for extra studies or spent some time together. She politely excused herself from them whenever they spoke to her about the guys or the guys who were hitting on her. She never entertained her friends or herself to indulge with the topic of guys.

Once a guy crossed her on the corridor of the school and then stopped right in front of her and turned around. He looked at her, then lowered his eyes and said "I have been following you since long and I want to tell you that….."

Her right hand waved at his left cheek before he could finish his sentence while growling "You bloody pervert."

Everyone around was taken aback and she left that place with a red face.

This incident was so hyped that she was called to the principal's room. She did not utter a single word and was dismissed. That guy was suspended from school for a week. Her parents felt proud of her for keeping their trust intact.

A week later when that guy joined school, he came to her directly.

"Hey, Sayuri. Hi. I am really sorry for that day.", he apologized keeping his eyes down with repentance.

She turned her back towards him and was about to leave when he continued, "I have been following you since long to tell you that….", he said in a single breathe. She turned towards him and he continued "congratulations and thanks for being an inspiration to me. And I am really sorry for that day.", he turned around and left, leaving her tight-lipped.

She did not tell him anything and nor did she exasperate herself.

Her focus ameliorated with time and inducement from her mother and father. She completed her graduation and got through some of the top ranked B-schools of the country. All her dreams were falling in place to be a reality. She had always wanted to get through the top ranked B-schools and learn the best of the professional life and settle down. But the fate had decided something else for her.

Sayuri learnt every single household work and became a helping hand for her mother. She was always pampered by her as she lived more time with her than anyone else. Her mother always told her that her birth had changed their family life. Her birth had changed her father. Her birth had brought light in her family and her wishes had turned true because of her. She was terrified when she wondered what would have happened if it would not have been Sayuri in her womb. And she had told her daughter a million times, that she was the only reason for the change in her father and her family.

Sayuri was an amazing cook. She cooked really well and never disclosed it to anyone. Her brother was the victim of her new experiments. He would eat and never grumble about the food and would say "Sayur, it was awesome. Try something new next time."

Unfortunately, unfortunate things happen. One day, she was in the kitchen when his father returned back from his office. Her mother opened the door for him and she was busy preparing "gajar ka halwa" for her father in the kitchen.

'Where is Sayuri?", he asked her while removing his footwear.

"She is preparing your favourite dish.", she replied with pride. Mothers always want their daughters to be self-sufficient and the best at whatever they do.

"How the hell did she learn cooking?", he slapped her while asking.

"Who let her get into the kitchen? It's not her age to get into the kitchen. How long has she been cooking? Why didn't you reveal this to me ever?" he asked while beating her.

Sayuri came from the kitchen hearing the yell of her father. Before she could say or do anything, she found her beloved mother had lost her sense and bleeding. She opened the door and took her to the hospital in a rickshaw. She got her admitted and hid the fact by saying it to be an accident. She never revealed this incident to anyone, not even to her brother or else he would have detested their father. She was discharged from the hospital after three days with the stitches. Sayuri stayed at the hospital with her mother without taking a bath or eating proper meals.

The mother and the daughter ate together when they reached home. She stayed by her till she recovered completely. She took care of her meals, her medicines, and her health till she was fit again like a horse. Sayuri knew that the love of her father for her made him arrogant and she could not risk her mother's life for this.

Instead of taking admission in the best of the college, she took admission in a nearby college which was 3-4 hours distance by bus so that she could come down to her home whenever she felt like. Her father insisted her to take admission in the best college and he promised her that he would not harm anyone. However she did not believe herself and she had already decided to enrol at nearby college as there was no college in her town.

She went home every weekend keeping her projects and assignments aside and spoke to her mother every day, whenever she was free. The conversation lasted from seconds to hours depending upon her classes. She had taken a vow to take care of her mother and keep her unscathed from this society, from this world and especially from her father. Her father never went against her and that incident did not affect her love or respect for her father. However it strengthened the bond between her and her mother.

She came down to the city of illusions looking out for a job and within a week she grabbed a job. After two weeks, she forced her father to get a transfer to this city. After a month, she was here in this new city with her mother and father. Her little adorable brother stayed back because of his studies.

This city, the new city for her where she had been earlier on her vacation to meet her relatives but now she shifted here, completely, with her parents. Some called it city of dreams, some called it as the city of happiness, some called it the city of struggle, some called it the city of illusion, some called it the city of luck, and she called it the city of marathon. She saw people running everywhere, every time. They never rest, they just ran either to catch a train or a bus or an auto or a cab or to reach office on time or to leave office. She found indefatigable people who ran and ran only for their survival. But she was content because she knew that she would never survive, she would never spend her life, and she would live her life.

She told many times to herself, *"It's my life, I will live my life the way I want."*

And this is what she would do in this marathon city. She would live her life, make her dreams a reality, fulfil all her wishes, and enjoy her life to the core as no one had ever done before. She felt free like a bird as she entered in to the world of professionalism, she felt complete as she had her parents with her and she felt content as she could foresee her career which would give wings to her covets.

She felt within herself every time that it's her life and now she could live her life the way she had lived with some more spice and some more colours.

"It's her life and no one has the rights to mess with her life.", the nature echoed.

He was all home, lost in thoughts and was enjoying his buoyant mood. He was so much into the feeling of love and into her thoughts that he did not text or call her. He was into a state of soliloquy. It was almost afternoon when he came out of his dream world to the world of reality. He realised that he had not been to his office nor had he informed his boss about it. He had also missed many calls and texts when he saw his phone.

He ignored all the calls and texts but Sayuri's. He had missed 18 calls and had not replied to 23 texts. And the last text showed "Where are you? Please reply ASAP. I am really getting worried about you."

He dialled her number instantly without missing a second.

"Hello?", she inquired.

"Sorry." he apologised.

"What the heck? You took the hell out of me. Where the hell were you since morning? Why did not you reply to my calls or texts? Do you want me to live in a state of panic? I am unable to concentrate on anything and was about to leave office in a few minutes." she questioned and said.

"Sorry sorry sorry sorry sorry. I am really sorry, Baba. I am really sorry. Please calm down.", he tried to pacify her.

"What calm down? What sorry? Do you know what I was going through since morning?", she was unstoppable.

"Ok. Relax. Chill. I will tell you. Wait."

"You know what?"

"Hmm?"

"I love the way you say "hmm", I would love to listen to your "hmm" when I will be on my death bed."

"Ssshhhh…. Let's live first then we will think of dying. We have just started living and we have to do so many things together, live our life to the fullest and love the life to the core in every possible way. Don't talk about death. Neither is it the right time nor I want this time to come till we are centenarians."

"Hmm.", she agreed, and inquired, "Where were you since morning?"

"I slept a bit late and woke up late as usual. I was so lost in thoughts that I forgot to go to the office and even I did not inform my boss. Secondly, the phone was in silent and I was so much into the last evening that I did not realise that I have a phone with me as I was talking to you in my mind."

"Liar."

"No. Seriously. I was completely lost and when I realised, I saw your texts and calls and called you up without skipping a more beat."

"Okay. I believe you."

"Thank you for believing me, Ma'am. And I love you, Saaya."

"I love you too.", she whispered.

"Why are you whispering?"

"I am in office. Don't you know that?"

'Ahaa…. Then it's the right time to pull your legs. I love you, sweetheart."

"Stop it na…. Please.", she requested as she could not speak properly in the office.

"Stopped. What are your plans for the day?"

"I am in office till evening. I probably will be a bit late as I am overloaded with work. And will be meeting my sweets at the bus stop in the evening as usual."

"Great. That's an awesome thing to listen to. I am reaching your office in half an hour."

"Why?" she inquired.

"Can't you just say "yes" and come without asking so many questions?"

"You know that I have so much work that I can't even leave office before eight. I am so over loaded and just because of you I can't even work since morning. You ruined my whole morning without letting me work."

"You were only saying that you would have left office if I would not have responded or called you up. Right?"

"Right, but…."

"But nothing. I am reaching your office in some time and we are going out for lunch. That's it."

"Please try to understand. I can't. I have so much work."

"I will be waiting for you. It's up to you whether you want to come or not."

"No, I won't be able."

"I am not forcing you. But I will be waiting for you. See ya. Tc."

"Sweets, no."

"Ta ta", and he dropped the call.

She was happy and stressed. She was happy as she would be going out with him for lunch. They would probably go out to live some special time, where she could see the setting sun with him and the rising moon. She was really stressed as she could not ask her boss to leave office because of the work pressure. She was over loaded with her own work and her boss' work.

Her boss hardly worked and distributed all her work among her team members. She gave most of her work to

Sayuri as she worked in a streamline way and maintained the data properly. She received all her work within the timeframe from Sayuri and took the credit for the work. She also took over the incentives of the work done by Sayuri. She simply passed her time with her colleagues or over the phone talking to her friends or family. She exploited Sayuri by asking her to come early and leave office late. Sayuri was over-burdened and reduced weight over the period.

He reached at her office half an hour later and texted her that he was waiting for her. She asked him to wait for some time as she was stuck with some errand handed by her churlish boss. He did not call her up and an hour passed by. He never liked to wait nor he loved to keep anyone wait.

She came running and apologised to him while panting.

He held her hands and asked her to calm down. She stood there for some time releasing her hands from his.

"What?" he asked as he felt awkward when she released her hand.

"Nothing. I am not comfortable with this. Anyone around might see and I don't like that." she replied while catching her breathe.

"Okay. Drink some water.", he said handing her the bottle of water which he had bought while waiting for her.

She drank some water and stood for a moment to catch her breathe. He observed the way she took the bottle from him, opened the cap, drank water, threw the bottle in the trash bin and stood silently without uttering a single word. He thought how civilised she was, how beautiful she was, how could she be so polite. Anyone would have thrown the empty bottle on the road instead of walking till the dust bin and doing a favour to their own self and to the society. Was she showing off or was she so civilised?

The honk of the cab disturbed his thoughts. He stopped the cab and both of them got inside the cab and headed towards Kobe's.

"How do you know that I love sizzlers and that too in Kobe's?", she asked.

"You had told me almost a year or two before that you had been to Kobe's with your colleagues and you loved the sizzlers over there. I wanted to go there with you to have sizzlers."

"I envy your memory and I should better remember what I say to you so that you won't take advantage of me." she teased him.

"Not exactly. I don't remember most of the things and besides you have got a great memory. I forget most of the important stuff which you will know slowly and slowly with time. You mostly will start shouting at me then. I am ready for that though."

"Hey, no need to be so serious."

"I am not. Not even a bit. I am sorry if my voice seemed so." He said while crossing his fingers with hers. "I don't want to leave you ever in my life. Not even for a single moment. And you don't even dare to leave me ever. Love you, Saaya," he said this with a silent smile and a drop of tear rolled down his cheek and fell on her little finger.

"What happened? Why are you crying?", she inquired while kissing her cheek.

"I believe I am completely in love with you irrespective of if you believe it or not. I am just requesting you not to leave me ever."

"Don't be so emotional. Everything will be fine.", she assured him and they reached her favourite restaurant.

"Let's hop in. I am famished."

He opened the glass door for her and entered after her. She guided him the route and they went up climbing the narrow and stiff stairs. He was glad that he was after her to take care of her. She chose a corner seat and he sat exactly opposite to her. He did not like the ambience of the restaurant as it had a dull colour on the wall and the floor was not mopped properly. No one but they were there on that floor.

"Why are you sitting there? Come here. Sit next to me.", she commanded with a touch of politeness.

He obeyed her like the officers obey to the commands given by their commanding officers in army.

She held his hands and said, "I want you to be there with me every time. Just beside me. I do not want you to walk or stand ahead or behind me. I do not want you to sit in front of me. I do not want you to sleep facing towards the other end. I just want you to be there with me, next to me, so that I can hold your hands whenever I want and feel you within me and console my own self that you are never going to leave me and are always close to me. Don't ever leave my side. Just be there beside me. Okay?"

"Now you are being emotional. Don't. I am holding your hands because I never will leave it. I will fight….", he was interrupted by the waiter who had brought two glasses and kept in front of them and filled water till the rim of the glasses.

"What would you like to have, sir?"

"Would you like to have veg. or non-veg.?" she asked me.

"Order whatever you want to. The day is all yours.", he replied.

"A veg sizzler with two hot gulab jamuns." she ordered. "How much time will it take?" she inquired.

"20 minutes, ma'am.", he said and left.

"Well, you were saying something.", she asked him to continue the talk which was interrupted by the arrival of the waiter.

"Yeah, I was saying that I will fight with….", and again he was interrupted. This time he was not interrupted by the arrival of any guests or the waiter, but by Sayuri whose lips were on his. His eyes were closed and thoughts were shattered by then. After a moment, she freed him and asked him to continue but his mind was blank by then. He never had kissed anyone and he felt as if a certain volt of current had passed through him when his eyes were closed.

He gave a silent smile to her and could not utter a single word. He drank some water and thanked her for kissing him. It was his first experience and it was an incredible experience. The feeling was indescribable for him. He was in the world of ecstasy. He sat there holding her hands trying to control his heart beats which had gone high enough and he could feel the beats and listen to its' rhythm.

The order had arrived and was placed in front of them. The waiter brought two plates out of which one was removed and only one plate rested on the table. He served the sizzlers, filled the glasses, kept the hot gulab jamuns next to the plate and left.

She took a spoonful of rice and put it in his mouth and then she took one. Before she could do anything else, he took one spoon and gulped one of the gulab jamuns just like kids swallow ice-cream without giving any thought or looking around.

"You know what?", she asked.

'Hmm?"

"Gulab jamuns are desserts which are supposed to be eaten after the main course."

"I know that but it's hot and irresistible, just like you.", he replied without thinking.

"What? What did you just say?"

"Nothing. I mean you are definitely way beyond that. You are beautiful, you are my shadow, you are a part of my life, you are…."

"Ok ok ok. Stop. I understood. You might have grown up but you are a kid. I love you, my sweets.", she said and kissed him again.

They finished their lunch, followed by a dozen more gulab jamuns which were gulped by him obviously. They both fought over paying the check and finally she won and made the payment.

"Where are we heading now?", she asked.

"I am done with my part. I wanted you to come here to have lunch with me and I did. It's your turn now."

'You are good at passing the ball to the other court. I should take care of it henceforth."

"As you wish." he replied.

"Let's go to your room as I want to be with only you, without being disturbed by anyone, not even by the sounds of an engine or a chirruping bird."

"Alright, missy. Your wish is my command."

They again booked a cab to go to his room.

"Did you like the sizzler?", he asked.

"There is no point asking this, sweets. You know that is my favourite place for sizzlers and I loved it much more just because of you, as you made it special today. Thank you for making the day so special after ruining my morning."

"I am sorry about that. I was completely lost and was in la la land."

"It's ok. No need to apologise. I am glad that you made this plan and asked me to leave office. I am so stressed these days with my professional life."

"Why don't you leave this job and look out for another option. Why are you listening to your boss who is doing nothing?"

"I am not doing this job for her or for anyone else. I am continuing with this job because I like this job. I am enjoying this job to the core. I left my first job within a year because I was not getting to learn much and I had reached my saturation point. I am learning something new every day which will help me in my career. I can never think of leaving this job until I get some exciting opportunity which will make me feel that I will enjoy and learn more than this job."

"Why are you keeping your health at stake for this?"

"Sweets, this is the time to stake everything at risk for career. Do you think that I can stake my health for my career after 8-10 years? We have to take care of other things then. I have to get stability in my career so that I can enjoy my life then. Got it?" she made him understood.

"You should have been a teacher or a professor. You are really fantastic at making others understand your point." he appreciated her.

They have reached his apartment and she again insisted to pay the cab driver. She thanked him after paying him.

"Why do you thank everyone? I saw you thanking that waiter, the cab drivers, the bus conductors, the shop-keepers, everyone. Is it really required to thank everyone around?", he asked her with eagerness.

"What if I say "Yes"?"

"Then I would like you to explain it to me." he replied while unlocking the door.

He stayed in the ground floor of an old apartment with a bedroom and a kitchen. They entered into the room, she removed her shoes while closing the door behind them and he switched on the light.

There was a mattress lying on one corner of the room with his laptop and charger over. A cupboard resting itself with all his dresses, novels and documents inside it on one corner and a shoe rack just behind the door. There was only a refrigerator in the kitchen and an induction cooking gas along with some jars and utensils. The floor was mat finished and the room was painted in light yellow.

"Before answering your question, I would like to say that you have maintained your room pretty well. Generally, guys don't keep their rooms so clean and well-maintained."

"I feel weird when the room is not clean, although I am a lazy fella, and I do not know how many times you had been to guys' rooms?", he teased her.

She frowned at him and hugged him tightly. He held her in his arms and she rested her feet on his and kissed him intensely. He did not feel like leaving her and she did not have any intention to be released from his clutch. Their emotions were intervened when her phone rang. She kept the phone on silent and returned back to him.

He was lying on a mattress which was covered with a blue bed sheet and a neatly folded blanket which was kept on the bottom of the mattress. She came back laid beside him and then rested her head on his chest, listened to his beats and he fondled her hair.

"Why do you have so less furniture in your room?"

"I don't like furniture or stuffs which lessen the importance of a room or make it crowded. I love the room as it is with only the necessary stuffs. Unnecessary stuff not only make the room look like a junkyard, it also takes the beauty away. I have got all the necessary stuffs which I need to live my life. Why should I overburden this room and myself with the things which I don't need and waste time in cleaning and maintaining? I believe that the positive energies not only lie within our self, it also lies around us. We just have to attract these to us and more spacious the room is, more the positive energies flow within the room. Besides, it's no more my room or your room, it's our home. I know that it's not yet a home but we will make it. I have always dreamt of having a small home in a big piece of land near a mountain or a lake side. We will have it one day and we will stay there with no intervention by anyone."

"I need it to be white in colour. I have always thought of having a white home. White has to be there inside the home and even outside.", she added.

"Done. It will be a white coloured small home in a big piece of land in an isolated place where we will be intervened by the nature only.", he summarized.

"Hmm….", and she continued, "from where did you copy that poem which you sent me last night?"

"Shall I lie or tell you the truth?"

"Truth, please."

"From my restless mind to the keypad of the phone."

"Liar, you are."

"Google it then.", he mocked as she googled everything she required.

"You write well. You should continue with that. You should never stop writing. I would like to read you every time, sweets."

"I blog."

"Do you? Why didn't you ever tell me?"

"You never asked me. And besides, don't ask me to post this in my blog as it was especially for you and I will not post this."

"Ok, I won't ask for that and thank you so much for making my morning then disintegrating it completely and then making it the best."

"Hmm. And now let's come back to our point of discussion. Why do you thank everyone?"

"Well, it's just the perception. I feel like thanking, so I do."

"I won't ask you if you don't feel like revealing because this is not an answer expected from you by your own self."

"Nothing like that. I love to thank everyone and everything around for helping me at given point of time. I thank the air for letting me survive, I thank the food for keeping me healthy and taking care of my body by increasing its' immunity system."

"You thank the food for taking care of your health. Do you know what have you become, what your health is?". He intervened with a serious note and an intention of mocking her.

"Sweets, no jokes please." she said with a strict tone.

"Sorry".

"Well, I thank every single cell of my body, I thank every single stranger for giving me a reason to smile or feel happy, I thank every single non-living thing for helping me to live my daily life. I thank to myself for my thoughts or whenever I help someone or my body or my body parts or billions of neurons or my voice or bones for making me what I am today. I thank my parents, my boss, the trees, the automobiles, the electronic gadgets, the internet, the entertainment industry, the fruits and vegetables, the dresses and the accessories, the millions of people who work for my living."

"Who works for your living?" he questioned.

"I wear this pair of clothes which initially came from a cotton plant which was raised by a farmer and then sold to some trader and that cotton was bought by a dress manufacturing company where so many people work to make this pair of clothes look so beautiful, so that when I wear it I feel confident and smart. Yes, my dresses have an effect on my confidence level. My confidence level goes down when I feel that my dress looks dull. Starting from the cotton soil, I thank the soil to the farmer to the cotton plant to the vehicles to the machineries to the retail outlets to all the people who are involved in this process."

"Don't you pay for that? Do they give you just like that without taking money from you? Every single person is paid for his/her effort. Then why do you thank?"

"It's not about money, sweets. It's about gratitude. Gratitude is the only thing which lack in people. They are not grateful for whatever good is happening in their life but they always blame for whatever goes wrong. That's what the problem with these human beings are. Gratitude is a positive thing. The more gratitude you bestow upon, more positive energy will engulf you, you will feel happier, and you will attract more things which will make you more grateful. Being grateful is just an act, just like the thoughts. You can't run away from it. If you thank at certain times, then why don't you thank all the time for every beautiful thing which happen in your life? That's what I don't understand. I don't care who says what. What I care is whether I live my life in my terms or not."

"Thank you, Saaya. Thank you so very much and I am really thankful to the nature or the universe or whatever is there for introducing you to me and letting me to be with you and letting you see my dreams through your eyes and making it as our dream. Thank you so much."

She faced towards him and hugged him and he stroked her hair. She was breathing heavily and he was feeling exceptional by her love and care.

She liked his thoughts of a home with minimum required furniture and his dream of a small home which became theirs when she revealed the white home to him. Her thoughts were completely filled with their future.

"You know what?", he blocked her thoughts instantly.

"Hmm?"

"I love the way you say "hmm" too. I even love your hair and the way it smells. I love your voice. I love your eyes, those are the most beautiful pair of eyes I have ever seen. I love your set of teeth, those are the perfect set of teeth." he stopped.

"And?", she asked.

"I love the way you speak. I love the way you think and the way your thoughts are. I love the way you respond. I love the way you pamper me. I love the way you hold my hands. I love the way you stay beside me. I love the way you cuddle me. I love the way you make me understand."

"And?" she asked him instantly as he stopped. She did not want him to stop. She just wanted him to speak. He sounded so sincere and so unadulterated that she could not resist her ears. She was pleading him with her unspoken words to continue. He was making her a woman, his woman whom he will never leave, with his words whom he loved so much. He was so true to her that he was saying everything from the abyss of his heart.

"I love your skin. I love your breathe which keeps seducing me every time. I love the way you hug me. I love the way you kiss me. I love the way you see my dreams through your eyes."

"It's no more yours or mine, it's ours. Remember?" she interrupted and reminded him what he had said earlier.

"Yes, I do. I wanted to check you out. I wanted to know whether you remember or not and you have got a sharp memory. I had told you, you remember?", he said while giggling.

"Ya, I do and you should better accept that you did not remember that and now you are checking me out sort of."

And he burst into laughter as she stated the fact and he knew that she understood him completely.

She joined him and they both laughed out loud till their jaw ached. It was time for her to leave and neither of them wanted to leave each other. It was real fun for them being with each other.

"Listen, Saaya."

"Hmm?"

"I am thankful to you for making my day and I hope I made your day too. In short, I hope our day was awesome and I am thankful to both of us for that."

"Good. It's the perfect way to show your gratitude. You are a fast learner."

"It's just because of you, teacher."

She giggled. She was sitting on the mattress and he was resting his head on her lap. She was stroking his hair and he had crossed her left fingers with his right and covered it with his left.

"I am really happy to have you in my life. You probably can never imagine. I will fight with you, I will cry with you, I will share my happiness with you, I will love you to the core, I will care for you, I will bug you with my unending valueless talks, I will bore you with my disgusting actions, I will share every piece of my life with you, I will shout at you and will ask you to leave me, I will avoid you and I will not even speak to you. You won't like when I will shout at you or fight with you or ask you to leave or when I will make you feel ignored but remember that I won't be able to live without you. Never leave me."

"Sweets, don't think much. I will go through your blogs and I have to leave now.", she said.

He got up, so did she and they got ready to leave. He hugged her tightly without letting the air pass through them. She could feel his heart beats and he could feel her breathe. He was dismayed that she had to leave. She asked him not to come with her as she could manage to go. He came outside and bid her goodbye when she got into the cab.

They chatted whenever they had free time and spoke whenever they could. They whispered at night and he loved her breathe which was seductive. She loved his voice and the way he pronounced "Saaya". He used to sleep during their calls most of the time and sometimes she did too. She loved his snores and he loved her breathe. He could do anything to feel her breathe when she was around. Her breath was so voluptuous.

He travelled throughout the day and moved through the nights with each other's texts, calls and evening meetings. He always waited for her call when she was out of the office till she reached the bus stop. He waited for her call during the lunch hour, and he waited for her call at night, even if he missed her and her calls. She missed his texts, his aesthetic voice, his interruption throughout the day while she was busy with her work.

◆━◈━◆

"Hey, sweets.",
"Hmm?"

"Let's go to marine lines tomorrow evening. I have been thinking of going there with you since long."

"Sure. Shall we go now? It's only 19:00 hours."

"Not today. Tomorrow?"

"Sure. At?"

"6:30."

"Done. I will see you tomorrow sharp at 18:30 hours. Please don't delay."

"Why do you always calculate time in 24 hours format? It sounds so cheesy."

"Well, I believe that I have only twenty four hours in a day. I don't have twelve hours of AM and twelve hours of PM. I have to plan my daily life as 24 hours in a day. I get confused when I divide the time into two. I can't divide certain things in my life."

"Like?"

"The love for you." he said instantly without a thought as if he was waiting for her to ask since ages so that he could reply.

"Stop flirting around every time.", she said.

He was excited about the idea of being with her the whole evening on the beach. They would look at the setting sun, the rising moon, feel the cool breeze, and speak a lot with their unspoken words while cherishing each other's company in nature's lap.

———◆———

He reached the bus stop by 18:00 hours and waited for her. He did not want her to wait in case she came early. He did not call or text her as he knew that she would be busy wrapping up her works.

His phone vibrated after fifteen minutes, and the text showed "Sweets, I will be late by ten minutes." He replied "Ok" with an annoyance. He kept waiting looking towards the gate of her office building and there was no sign of her. He called her, which went in vain. The minute hand crossed the digit twelve in his wrist-watch and he was exasperated. He had waited for more than half an hour for her from the said time. He had been waiting for more than an hour just to ensure that she would not have to wait and there was no sign of her. He was vexed by this.

Just as he took his phone out of his pocket to drop a text to her while the phone buzzed.

"Yeah?", he asked.

"I am so sorry, sweets. I was tied up with so much work that I could not respond to you and at the very last moment when I was about to leave, my boss turned up and explained me the things which I have to do tomorrow." she explained to him.

"Where shall we go now? Home?", his voice was filled with irritation.

"I said I am sorry."

"You don't need to be. Why are you sorry? What are you sorry for? You could have said earlier. At least I would not have waited for more than an hour like a fool." he said with a high pitch.

Whenever he lost his mind, he lost control over his voice. He could not control the volume of his own voice and she never liked someone talking to her with a high pitch.

"Calm down. Don't shout.", she requested.

He did not say anything. He knew that their plan was ruined and the evening was spoiled. She looked around for a cab and then hopped into it and he followed her. She asked the driver to go to marine drive. She held his palms in hers and rubbed it slowly without uttering a single word. She then squeezed his hands and hugged him.

"Sweets. Listen na.", she said with a soft seducing tone.

He neither responded nor looked at her.

"I am sorry, sweets. You know how my boss is and you know I never like to keep you on wait. You know what?",

"Hmm?", he responded automatically.

"I love the way you say "hmm"." She said and kissed her right cheek. "Are you still mad at me, hottie?"

He looked at her and hugged her tightly and whispered, "Why do you keep me waiting when you know that I don't like to wait at all? I was waiting for you since 18:00 hours so that you would not have to wait if you come early. I understand that you have work and we are not going out every day. At least you could have managed."

They got down at marine lines and sat there facing towards the sea, feeling the breeze across their faces. The intention of enjoying the setting sun and rising moon was lost. Many couples were busy locking their lips, some resting on others lap, some lying next to each other as if they were counting the number of stars in the clear blue sky or finding out the pattern, some filling their lungs with smoke, children playing with their parents, some elderly people enjoying the gust of air and some jogging while some of the most expensive cars were running on the road.

They were sitting next to each other holding each other and she was resting her head on his shoulder looking towards the sea. The water was dancing to the tune of the wind at a distance from the shore. Waves near the shore were singing while rubbing themselves against the stones. The road had divided the place into two. One part was miraculously taken care of by the nature herself. The other part was erected with skyscrapers and maintained by the so-called two-legged creatures which were known as the God's greatest creation as they have the ability to think, to tame, and to do miracles by inventing incredible instruments or contrivance.

It seemed, to her, as if human beings and nature were just standing next to each other and were completely prepared if ever one declared a war against the other. She adored nature and was pondering over the actions of the nature.

"Have you ever seen the calamity or anger of nature?", she asked.

"In reality? No. On Television? Many a times. Why? What happened?"

"Nothing in specific. Just remembered the catastrophe. Almost a decade ago, I had reached home from school when the sky was covered with dark clouds and it was the darkest night I have ever visualised till today. It was five in the evening, and there was no sign of the sun or the moon anymore and the wind was speeding up with its speed. My father had not reached home then and bro was home with mother that day as he was not feeling well. My mother and I were worried about father as it was about to rain. It's not the rain which was bothering us, it was the nature's expression. After a few minutes, my father reached home and he said that there was a low pressure and the meteorologists had forecasted that it would rain heavily.", she looked at him and asked, "are you bored?"

"No. Not at all. I am listening to you. Continue, please."

"After half an hour or so, the wind blew heavily and it started raining. We closed all our windows and doors and panicked hearing the growl of the wind. It seemed as if it would take everything away with it and not leave anything behind. There was no electricity and the phone was dead by night. We could not move out and see what's happening. The following day I just asked to open the door to see the on-going and he agreed. I opened the door slowly and I saw that all the trees were lying flat on the earth, wherever I glanced, I saw nothing but water. Trees and plants were swimming in it and the nature had decided not to leave any stone unturned. It continued for three days and after three days we were surrounded by water. We could not move out of the house. Roads were blocked with the trees. There was no electricity or phone to get the news of the outside world. Government declared a week holiday for us. Later on, father came back with the news that the nature took its' vengeance by destroying thousands of villages, killing millions of people and shattering billions of properties. We were lucky enough to be alive. I felt that day as if I would have died like others but no, I was supposed to live and if I have to live then I will not spend it, I will live my life irrespective of any odds.", she breathed heavily and held his hands tightly.

He was listening to her intently without intervening her. He was all ears to understand the meaning behind the words. He loved her more when he found she was like him.

She just believed in living her life and that's what mattered to him. Live life, not SPEND.

"Saaya?"

"Hmm?",

"Have I ever said you that I love you?"

She thought for a moment and replied, "No. Never."

"I love you, my Angel. I love you much more than yesterday and less than tomorrow.", he confessed.

"And I just love you. I don't know how much but I love you and that's enough for me."

"Thank you. Thank you so much for being a part of my life and letting me be a part of yours."

He remained silent for some time and looked into the sea as if he was trying to measure the depth of the sea.

"Where are you lost, sweets?" she asked finding him lost.

"Well, I don't want to hide anything from you. I want you to know everything about me to avoid all future misunderstandings."

"You are panicking me.", she confessed.

"I don't want you to hear anything about me from anyone else but myself. It hurts when you listen something from another person whom you hardly trust about the person whom you trust more than yourself."

"Sweets, will you please tell me? I am worried now."

"I had a few many girls in my life. I never hugged or kissed any of them even but I wanted you to know this."

She was deadpan.

"Why didn't you tell me earlier?"

"Never had a suitable time."

"Were you close to any of them?"

"Mentally? Yes. Physically? No." he revealed the facts.

"Will you go back to any of them who you were close with?", she again became inquisitive.

"If you would have asked me initially when we met a few years ago, I would have said "Yes". We are in a relationship since a few months and have known each other since few years. If you ask me whether I will go back to any of them now if anyone turns up then I will say that I am completely addicted to you. I don't want to leave you or live without you." he said with a low voice.

"Are you sure that you are never gonna cheat on me or leave me ever in your life?"

"I can assure you that I will never leave you. Besides, I don't need to answer your first question. Ask your own self and if you feel that I will ever cheat on you, then this is the time for you to cut this stuff completely here and move on.", he said looking into her eyes.

"I am sorry for asking you that.", her eyes were full of tears when she apologised.

"Hey, Saaya. You don't need to apologise. I am sorry that I did not reveal this to you earlier. I should have but I was afraid that you would leave me and I did not want to leave you from my life, Angel. I was waiting for the perfect time. I am so sorry. Please don't cry. I can't see you cry." His eyes were wet then.

She wiped his eyes and hugged him tightly and whispered, "je t'aime."

"Je t'aime aussie."

His phone rang and he took out his phone. The phone had her wall paper while taking a photo. It wass a black and white photo of hers in which she was wearing a sleeveless top and holding a Nikon DSLR in her left hand and the right hand was focusing on the buttons to set the image while her left eye was concentrated on the image shown on the DSLR. She had sent this to him one night when he was going to bed and he spend the whole night dreaming about being with her after viewing this shot. It was one of her best prints which he looked at frequently. She looked fabulous in this still. He had thanked her many times for sharing this photo with her and complimented a million times for the way she looked. She seriously was looking terrific. It was incredible for him to accept someone looking so beautiful without any make-up. She looked so simple as if she was the Goddess of simplicity.

She hauled the phone from him when the phone displayed the name "Ashi".

She was aggrieved and asked with a rough tone, "Who is she?"

"I will tell you but receive the call first or else it will be missed. Please receive the call."

She had accepted him as her property and no one had the right to trespass. She was hurt when she saw such a name on his phone as it was unexpected. She had decided that she will burst out at the girl at the other end of the phone so that no one can dare to eye on her belonging. She was not insecure but possessive, a bit, which he could sense or she could be jealous, he thought.

She never wanted to speak to any of his contacts but this time she received the call.

"Who is this?", she bursted.

"Hello?", she heard a sweet voice coming out from the other end with a serenity.

"Who are you and why do you want to speak to him?", she asked with an uneven voice which he had never heard before.

"Okay. Calm down, please. So my surprise is ruined and you are no other than Saaya. Right, sweetheart?", the voice said.

She was shocked with this statement. She looked at him with a bewilderment and asked with her body language, "Who is she and how does she know me?". He looked at her and enjoyed her expression without replying and asked her to continue with the call.

"I ruined your surprise?", she asked with an astonishment, "I believe I am surprised. I don't know you, I have never heard about you and you hit the bull's eye by talking to me as if you had known me since ages.", she replied with a soft tone.

"That's right. I know you. Not much though but I do know you. You are in a lucky hand. And I thank you for taking care of this dumbo."

"Alright. Shall I get an opportunity to know the owner of the sweet voice?"

"You are flattering me. I had asked him not to say anything about me and I wanted to give you a surprise physically. However, the dumbo ruined it."

"How is that?", she inquired.

"I am coming this weekend and wanted to meet you personally and introduce myself to you. As the plan is ruined so let me introduce myself because you were introduced to me by him. I am Afsheen, a friend of his, rather he is my best friend, the one and only friend I can rely upon for anything. You don't have to feel insecure or jealous about me though.", she pulled Sayuri with her last statement.

"Okay. So I have someone I should be aware of. Is not it?" she mocked her.

"Is he around?" Afsheen asked.

"No. He took my phone and is speaking to someone."

"I knew it."

"Sorry?"

"That's what he does. He does not want to listen to our conversation for which he left us to speak without being intervened. He gives space to everyone."

"Oh!", she exclaimed.

"So, how are you and how is life?"

"I am great. When are you coming next week?"

"Weekend. And you are booked. No excuses, no justification."

"I am afraid that I will not be able to meet you, Afsheen. I will be out of the city. I am going to attend one of my best friends' wedding. I wish I could meet you. But I promise we will meet next time."

"I don't believe in next time because I am not sure about the next time. No issues though."

He came slowly from the behind and dragged the phone from her.

"What the hell are you talking about me? Don't you dare say her anything behind my back." he said while laughing over the phone.

"I told her everything about you and she is irate and you're gone, my dear dumbo."

He looked at her and said, "I will take care of her but you are gonna see your doomsday when you turn up."

She laughed and he bid her a bye and disconnected the call.

"You both are pretty close to each other?", she asked.

"Yes, we are. School buddies, you know?"

"Hmm. Why didn't you tell me about her earlier?"

"She had asked me not to tell you about her as she wanted to surprise you by introducing herself. She is coming next week and we all will have fun. I know that it's not possible for you to come over the weekends but I would be really happy if you could make it. Don't turn me down. Please.", he requested.

"I am sorry. I won't be able to make it. I am going to my hometown to attend my best friend's marriage. Do you remember my school buddy who is staying in Pittsburgh? Whenever she comes, she stays with me and she is here, since a month, for her marriage and we have not met yet. I can't miss her marriage and I am going there only for a day as my boss is not approving my leaves. She is so mean. She takes leave whenever she wants but not letting me. How could someone be so mean?"

"When are you leaving?" He asked with a shock as he was unaware of that.

"Sorry, sweets. I forgot to tell you. I am going on Friday evening and will come back on Sunday night. My little innocent bro will accompany me while coming."

He was disheartened. He had planned to go to movie, the theme park, have lunch together and live the moment with the two most important people of his life. His plans were ruined. He was dejected by her plans.

"What happened? What's wrong? I am sorry for not letting you know earlier."

"It's Okay. No hassles. You have fun there and don't get lost completely in the merry making. Do remember that someone is away from you, thinking about you all the time." He said by bringing a fake curve on his face with a pair of desolate eyes.

"Ahh…. Don't be so dismayed. I thought I had told you but I realised now that I did not tell you. I am sorry, sweets."

"It's Ok, Saaya. I understand. I actually had made some plans as I thought you would be here and we all would have fun. She called me up to confirm that she had booked the tickets for next week. She is coming to meet you especially and she had not been here since long. She comes here just to meet me and this time she is taking time out from her work to meet you, I am not the reason for her arrival. I will take care of her thoughts. Nothing to worry about. And stop apologising now."'

"I wish I would have told you earlier. I am really feeling bad now. She is coming to meet me and I won't be there."

"You don't need to feel about anything. It's alright."

"Why don't you ask her to cancel the tickets and book it for next weekend?"

"She won't do that as she won't have time in the next week. I know the way she manages her work. She will come next week if I say but I won't say as I know her work pressure like I know your boss."

She did not say anything afterwards. They never had miscommunication. They were always open to themselves but this was an aberration.

She was terribly hurt and so was he. Apart from them, Afsheen's plans were also smashed by Sayuri's unanticipated plans.

———◈———

A Muslim guy skipped his beats for a Hindu beauty in the 80s. The guy belonged to an open-minded business family where everything was welcomed. They did not have any feelings for any religion or festivals. They observed the festivals of all religions with their friends of different religions. They were adored and respected in their community as well as the society for their generosity. They believed their Almighty had bestowed so much blessing upon them, so that they could help the society to make it a better world. They believed that endowment starts at home for which they serve their guests well. The guy was the only child and was sober and decent. He did not smoke or booze. He was a religious guy, respected elders and topped in all his exams and extra-curricular activities.

The girl's family was highly conservative. They belonged to a middle class family. She obeyed her parents, respected everyone and was loved for her soberness. She was soft-spoken and never lost her temper. She was good at studies. Not only her parents but also her family members had lots of hopes and expectations from her. They wanted a groom from their community who would be highly educated and from a respectful family to show their pride among their relatives and friends. She never wanted her parents to bend their head in front of anyone. She never did anything ever in her life to let her parents' head down in front of anyone. That was one of the major reasons her parents trusted her more than themselves.

Finally, she skipped her beats to take care of the beats of that guy. They met in the college garden and exchanged letters. There were no phones in those times to talk. They shared all their feelings. They celebrated festivals together.

She went on fasting during Ramzans and he stayed hungry on Shiv Ratris and other festivals. They managed it pretty well without being caught. Four years passed by and their college time came to an end. They knew that it was impossible for them to live without each other. She could not go against her parents. She couldn't let them down. She was afraid. She told him that she would commit suicide as she could not live without him and she could not let her parents down.

He finally revealed their relationships to his parents. They wanted to meet her parents and speak to them for their children's betrothal but he denied. He requested them not to do anything like that as it would hurt her. He could never do anything to hurt her. They asked him to elope with her and they would make all sorts of arrangements, legally. Although his parents were known for their generosity and had contacts with the high profiles, they never took advantage. They held their heads high every time.

Finally, they eloped and left for Europe. His parents had a small business there and he took care of it. He wanted to expand his father's business abroad. He finally got the chance to do so and his luck was there with him now, his wife. They both were happy and he felt like the king of the world. He gave time to his business and to his family i.e. his wife. He never neglected either. He was so much in love with her that he wanted her to join their business and supervise things. She initially denied but later on accepted and went to office. His actual intention of asking her to join his office was to have lunch with her and have a glance of hers rather than her photo. He was deeply in love with her and could not see her out of his eyes. Whenever he went out for business tours, she went with him. He wanted her to be with him so that she also could see new places along with him. Their business trips were basically recreational tours.

They were like one soul in two bodies. Their love was eternal and their bond lied in trust and transparency. She knew everything about his professional life and he knew about her thoughts. He never mistreated her but treated her as his mistress. She looked after him when he was exhausted or in a grumpy mood and he cooked for her when she was unwell. Their relationship was like water, a perfect combination of Hydrogen and Oxygen.

Exactly after two years, on the Valentine's Day, she gifted him the most precious gift of his life. She presented him the most beautiful gift, Afsheen. He could not resist his happiness. He distributed sweets to everyone in the hospital and kissed her for such a lovely and beautiful gift. He thanked her and the tears rolled down his cheeks.

She was not in touch with her parents since they were betrayed by their own blood. Whenever anyone asked them about her, they simply replied that their daughter died. After a year, no one cared to ask them about her. Besides, people never had time to spend time on one thing. They always looked for something new to speak about, spread rumour about and make fun of. They were mean and cheap. They never really cared about anything until and unless it happened to them. This is what society was where even your near and dear ones could leave you or make fun of you in your absence because they did not have the guts to speak on your face. Her parents were still in love with her. The emotions of love and tear were hidden by anger.

She mailed them their granddaughter's photo. They cried a lot when they saw their granddaughter. Afsheen looked totally like her mother. They went to her in-laws place and spoke to their daughter and son-in-law. Their in-laws welcomed them as if nothing had ever happened. They felt guilty about their deeds. They discerned their mistake and realised that the religion of humanity is way beyond everything. They found their daughter to be happy and all their angst vanished. They wanted to see their granddaughter but she was unsure about fulfilling her parents' wishes.

He cancelled all his professional plans for a week and booked tickets to their hometown for three of them. They came to India, took blessings from both their parents and for the first time, they had lunch together, keeping the religions and other despicable thoughts away. All of them were happy, mostly parents of Afsheen, as they were finally accepted by her parents and they thanked Afsheen for making all these happen.

Afsheen became an integral part of their love and life. He became very responsible for his family. Afsheen was born with the qualities of her parents. She was the best, simply the best, at everything. She never did anything which she did not like. If she laid her hands on anything, then she never let anyone take over her. No one dared to mess with her. She learnt self-defence to protect herself at the time of need. She learnt shooting as she found it to be interesting. She learnt horse-riding as she wanted to control them. She learnt art because she fell in love with nature. Her mind always dwelt, her thoughts were restless. She could not sit idle. She engaged herself with learning new things. She took her life as a game, a game to win and never to lose. She never lost to anyone or anything.

By the time, she was into her puberty, she looked like an angel. No one had ever dared to propose her because of her attitude. She was amiable, convivial, gregarious, sympathetic, benevolent, and easy-going however she knew how to maintain a safe distance from everyone who could take advantage of her. She always played safe and accepted her fault irrespective of how big or small it was. She never quantified a mistake by measuring it. A mistake was a mistake for her. She never made a mistake twice. She believed that a mistake was no more a mistake if it was repeated, it was a blunder and one should be penalised by self for committing a blunder. She didn't have enough time to punish herself for which she learnt from her mistake and remembered that forever.

She came to her native place with her parents after the completion of her higher secondary. Her parents wanted to expand their business here. She bent down and touched her grandparents feet when they initially met them. Her grandparents hugged her and adored her for her cultural etiquettes. They hugged their children for helping Afsheen to be so traditional. Yes, she was traditional yet modern in her approach.

When she was asked to stay back, study here and learn about the cultural values and learn about her motherland, she agreed. Her parents also agreed to her decision. They decided to stay back with her and visit France whenever required. The motive to stay back was to be with Afsheen as they could not live without her.

<hr />

Afsheen was enrolled in the school where he was studying. He was an old student of that school and everyone knew him for his voluntarism. He was gregarious, friendly, jovial and helpful. He was respected by his juniors and loved by his seniors and teachers.

The day she entered into the school, almost every guy's mouth fell apart. Boys felt as if the Goddess herself walking into their school premises. This Goddess was not the Goddess of education or wealth or love, this Goddess is the Goddess of Lust. She asked a guy where her class was and he could not utter a single word, the other one stammered and finally she got the proper reply from a girl. When she entered the classroom, the eyes of every guy's came out. Every single girl was jealous at the first sight as the guys forgot them and were staring at her.

He was sitting on the last bench as usual. He looked up at the chaos created by his mates, looked at her, scanned her completely within a jiffy and went back to his work. It always took him a jiffy to conclude the character of someone but he did not conclude anything about her as he was lost in his thoughts. Later that day, he realised that his seniors, juniors and class mates were after her. Everyone approached him to get some information about her. She had become a sensation and the point of attraction in the school on the very first day.

He waved at her with a smile when she was entering the classroom and he was going out of the class room after the break. She returned his smile with a "Hi".

"Afsheen.", she introduced herself by extending her hands to shake with his.

He shook hand with her without introducing himself and asked, "How's the day going?"

"Not that great yet. It seems as if guys had never seen a girl before.", she said with a sarcasm.

She had a different pronunciation. It took him a while to interpret her as he was not that great with foreign pronunciation. She read his mind and spoke slowly to avoid any miscommunication or misunderstanding.

"That's hilarious from your point of view and from my point of view they have never seen a girl like you."

"Are you hitting on me?"

"No intentions, missy. And no offence. Just stating the fact. I have no reason to flatter you but I should not miss the chance to compliment you. I don't care what you conclude."

"I like your guts and confidence too."

"I need to be excused now. I don't want you to like me though."

He bid her bye and she contemplated with his last sentence. None of the guys ever spoke to her like the way he did. Guys were after her every time and she always maintained a safe distance from them although she spoke to them and had fun with them. But he was different, he was mean and rude enough to speak to a girl like this. How can a guy, overall a guy, could speak to a girl like this, that to of the same age? The guys who looked at them talking to each other started enquiring about her. He was in no mood to say anything. He simply said that her name was "Afsheen" and within an hour the whole school, even the girls, knew her name. Most of the guys envied him for his guts. He could do anything and if he was challenged then there was no chance that he would not do. He could speak to the person who hated him, he could enter into the principal's office directly and ask her a day off for the whole class, he could say to the teacher that he was not worthy of teaching them.

She was a bombshell. She was straight-forward. She was far ahead of every single student in the school. No one matched her from any perspective. Everyone's eye was on her. It seemed to her as if she had become the celebrity of the school. Celebrities did not have any personal life. Wherever they went, the media, the people, their followers, their fans followed them and everyone's eye was on them. Similarly, she was watched by everyone. Eyes were watching all her steps and all her movements. She felt over-whelmed and conscious for so many eyes.

She returned from school with her chauffer who brought a BMW 7 series. Most of the guys stepped back realising her status, rather the BMW, thinking that she was not their cup of tea.

"How was your first day, sweetheart?" her father asked.

"Celebrity feeling."

"What do you mean?"

"You do not need to worry about me anymore. I am taken care of by more than thousand pairs of eyes. I feel as if there are so many people to take care of me in your and mom's absence." And she laughed.

"So everyone was watching you. How many guys spoke to you?", he asked.

They were free to talk about anything and everything. Their relationship lay in transparency and trust. That's what he had always believed to strengthen a relationship. Relationships are scattered when there is room for lying or hiding something just because one feels that the other one will feel bad. But they took care of emotions and egos without hurting the sentiments.

"Most of them stammered and behaved like dumb but one."

"Ahhaa…. Sounds fishy?" he said with a suspicion.

"Nothing like that, Dad. You know that. We met at the doorstep of the classroom during the break and just had an introduction."

"Are you sure that there wasn't anything special? You would not have remembered this if there was nothing exceptional about him. What's the matter, darling?", he asked. He knew his daughter just like he knew himself.

"I told him that I liked his guts as he dared speak to me and he replied that he did not want me to like him. I was taken aback with this reply. No one has ever replied to me like this. Also the funniest part was that he was unable to understand me for which I had to speak slowly to avoid any miscommunication"

"You both are going to be good pals.", he forecasted like a soothsayer.

"How can you say so?"

"Wait and watch, dear. Don't overstress yourself." he concluded.

They always exchanged a "Hi" or a "bye" whenever they met each other accidentally. He never came to her deliberately to speak to her or she never spoke to him as he was sitting in the last corner bench. They never had any feelings nor did they want to add one more contact to their list just for the sake.

They were just formal friends without any attachments or concerns. She excelled in her studies and co-curricular activities over the years as she used to do earlier. She turned many guys down and maintained healthy relationships with everyone around. Girls liked her because they were at least not insecure about her that she would snatch their boyfriends but talked behind her back as she did not give anyone a chance to go ahead of her either in studies or extra activities.

She could not get the attention of two of the teachers in her school life, one was Maths and the other one was Chemistry. He never scored a number less than full in Maths and he was so good at calculation that he never missed a digit or got it wrong when he was given to calculate in atomic numbers.

A five by six digits multiplication was given by the chemistry teacher once and he was challenged by his friend that he could not complete it before him. He accepted the challenge. He took a pen and a piece of paper and that guy took the calculator. He completed before him with cent per cent accuracy and he made it wrong using a calculator and from that day his name was changed to "Calculator" by the chemistry teacher. If she did not get the answer within a minute then she looked around for him and would state that, "My calculator is absent, I believe."

He never competed with her or anyone, just like others. He was content with his achievements and performance. She wanted to speak to him once to know him, to satisfy her curiosity but he never let anyone enter into his sheath. She was maintained a hand distance from him, by him. She knew that he could easily trespass anyone's sheath without seeking permission, without letting them know and without affecting himself and pacify the other one. He was so good at it, the best perhaps.

"Can I have a word with you?", she asked him once.

"Sure."

"I want to quench my curiosity."

"And what's that?"

"I am curious to know about you. I don't want to know what others are saying because you are not what they say, you are different. They are seeing what you are showing them, they are listening, what you want them to listen and they are speaking about you what you want them to speak."

"Listen, Afsheen.", he took her name for the first time, looked into her eyes, with a silent smile, as if he was penetrating through her heart to suss out her questions and continued, "You are not so close to me that I will tell you the truth nor am I so close to you that I will answer all your questions, whatever you want to know. I don't prefer to lie so it's better if you don't unwrap."

She understood that he was a tortoise. He had a tough shell and took his head out whenever he wanted to or else kept it inside the shell knowing that no one could break it. She never had a close friend of her age. She was lucky enough to have her parents who were her best friends, guides, philosophers. She had friends with whom she could have fun, go out for shopping, hang out, watch movies, crack jokes but she did not have a friend with whom she could rely upon just like she relied on her parents.

She felt lonely when her parents left her and went to France for business meetings. She spoke to them after leaving her school or during her break but their presence mattered a lot to her. They came back as soon as their meetings were over without delaying a minute. They had fun. They observed every festival, be it Eid or Diwali. They prayed to Allah and Krishna, there was a family of culture, togetherness and happiness.

He returned back from the practical class once because he had forgotten to take his geometric box with him. He was stunned to find Afsheen sitting at her place in the class room. No one else was there apart from the bags of the students.

Everyone was in the laboratory for their respective practical classes. Practical classes were really funny than the theories. You could get a chance to dissect a frog or a leaf in Biology practical, mix up different acids to find out the reaction and note it in Chemistry or take the measurements from different angles in Physics. It was fun.

"Hey, Ashi. What happened? What's wrong?, he asked her with a friendly and caring tone and the pet name came automatically.

"Nothing.", she replied looking down.

"Look at me."

She did not look at him. She was still looking down. He held her chin and raised her face up. Her eyes were wet although there was no sign of tears rolling down. Her eyes were looking down. She could not look at him directly. She had never revealed her emotions in front of anyone apart from her parents and for the first time, her sentiments were being revealed in front of this guy who had never let her peep into him.

"Hey, Ashi. Listen. Don't shed your tears. I know that shedding tears will make you feel comfortable and relaxed but this is not the time to do it. I don't want others to take advantage of you. Shedding tears is the sign of strength but this whole world says that only the weak cry. They don't know how much strength is required to cry. You need to have enough guts to cry but don't cry in front of people who don't know the meaning of tears and make fun of it. Never let anyone make fun of you for any damn reason. You know what your strength is and weaknesses are, no need to prove it to others. It's your life, live it the way you want not the way others want you to.", she heard him referring as "Ashi".

She wondered about him. Why is he being so nice to me? Is he like this to everyone or is he being courteous to me? Why didn't he answer me then and why is he expecting answers from me now? Why is he behaving as if we have known each other since ages and close to each other although he is speaking to me for the first time and never spoke to me rather than a "hi" or "bye"? Is he insane or is he the example of humanity?

"Will you stop thinking and tell me what's wrong with this beautiful young lady who is chased by so many guys?", he asked as if he read her mind and tried bringing a smile on her face.

"Nothing. I am serious."

"Well, I know that I am not so close to you that you would say me what's going on in your mind for which you are desolate but don't lie to me that there is nothing. I won't feel bad if you say that you don't want to tell me because we are not close enough. But remember, never lie to yourself. Never ever do that. When you get up in the morning, you see the mirror and in the mirror you see no one but you. The mirror taught me that I have no one in this world apart from my own self. I need to respect myself, obey myself and take care of myself."

"My parents."

"I know that you have your parents with you and they are always going to be with you. They are your best pals and always going to be. If they are not around then you don't have any reason to feel down. You are missing them and so are they. If they get to know that you are not feeling well then they will leave everything and come to you and never leave you alone which you are aware of. Do you want them to leave their business and be with you or do you want to leave your studies and be with them?

"Neither. How do you know about all these? Were you stalking me?"

"I don't have much time to do all these. I hear stuff when I socialise. I filter the data and store the required data in these grey cells. You are the talk of the town so it's obvious that I listen stuffs about you. So simple."

"What else have you heard about me?"

"I don't understand why people always want to listen about self?"

"Don't you consider yourself as a human being?"

"If this whole world is full of human beings then I am a cannibal and if this whole world is a bunch of some other stuffs then I would prefer to call myself as a human being."

"Wow…. You should meet my parents."

"I am not coming to meet your parents. I am not interested in getting married to you and I have wasted half of my practical class because of you. Shall we go to the class now?"

"No, you go. I won't. The teacher will start interrogating."

"You don't need to fear when I am here.", he said in a filmy tone and she laughed. He continued, "I will take care of that. Besides, so many guys must be looking around for you."

She could not resist her laugh now.

She spoke to him frequently since then and he came closer to her sheathing himself though. She found her friend whom she could rely upon and she shared about her life in France, her friends whom she still called, her classes, her horse-riding, the way her parents got eloped, her grandparents union and so on.

He listened to her attentively.

"I need a help.", he said once.

"Sure."

"I want to speak English like you."

"Your English is good. Why do you want to speak like me?"

"You are remarkable. You are freaking awesome."

"Then I will start finding out your mistakes if you don't mind."

"Definitely not. I will do whatever you want me to, Teach."

"You are in the right hands, my dear Student."

And they both burst into laughs.

She stayed sometimes at her maternal grandparents' place and sometimes at her paternal grandparents' place when her parents were not around. She learnt Mythology when she was at her maternal place and learnt about "the Quran" when she was at her paternal grandparents' place. She learnt everything about Hindu and Muslim religion to discover that Humanity is the best religion.

———◈———

"Hey, sweetheart, how are you?", asked her father.

"I am great, Pops. I missed you both so much.", replied Afsheen,

"What's cooking up? I am glad that you are happy." he asked observing her expressions.

"Nothing much."

"Are you sure?"

"Absolutely, my fortune teller."

"Okay. I understood. In love?"

"No, Dad. He is a best pal to rely upon. I am glad that he was there when I missed you both so much. Thank you for letting me be me."

"When are we meeting up then?"

"I don't know. He does not want to meet you. He said that he is not marrying me then why should you want to meet him."

"Interesting."

"When would you like to meet him?"

"How are you going to do that?"

"Don't worry, I will manage it."

"Let's meet tomorrow at dinner then. What do you say?"

"Perfect. Your wish is my command."

They both laughed aloud.

She left her Maths notes in his bag the following day deliberately so that he would come to her home. She called him up after leaving school to return her notes and help her with Maths as he was good at it.

He went to her place knowing that something was cooking up. He rang the doorbell when her mother opened the door.

He folded his hands to convey his respect and saw a man in his fifties whom he conveyed his respect in the same way. His respect was returned by them.

Her home was a big one, well-maintained. Their hall was the size of his home. There was a staircase in the middle of the hall connecting to the first floor. The kitchen was on the right side, a temple in front, a 80" LCD hanging on the wall left to him. It was a white house from outside and inside and the interior was fabulous. He thought how rich they wwere, they obviously are aristocrats. He wondered the number of people like him who were hired by them to work.

"Afsheen forgot her notes in the school and wanted me to return it to her.", he said to her father before they could ask anything.

"Would you like to have a cup of tea or coffee?", her mom asked ignoring his statement.

"No, ma'am. I don't prefer tea or coffee. A glass of water will do."

She returned in a few minutes with a glass of lemon juice. He gulped it and kept it on the table placed before him.

"Thank you, Ma'am. Is not Afsheen there?"

"She will be here in a couple of minutes. She is in her room.", her mom responded.

"How is the business going on, Sir?", he asked her father to keep his nervousness away from them and himself. He knew that he should not have asked him such a question but he did not get anything else to ask him.

"It's good. We recently came back from France."

"I know. How was your trip?"

"It was good and we missed our daughter a lot."

"She missed both of you a lot too." He said without giving a second thought.

His voice was friendly and anyone from a conservative family would have minded the way he spoke with them. They must have considered him a mannerless guy. However her parents appreciated him. She walked down the staircase and she was looking wonderful. Her hair were wet and she was wearing a blue trouser and a white top.

"Hey, sorry for the trouble. I forgot the notes and I wanted you to help me with Maths as you are a genius at it.", she said.

"Sir, can I speak to her for a minute?", he asked her father like an intrepid.

"Sure.", he was carried away by his guts and respect.

He took her to the corner of the room and whispered.

"Do you think me to be a fool? Stop acting now at least. When you told me that your notes are in my bag, I knew that you kept it deliberately so that I could come here. When I rang the doorbell, it seemed as if your parents were waiting for me. Why are you faking? You wanted me to meet them and I fulfilled your wish. There is no need to act now.", he said in a flat tone without any emotions.

She laughed after listening to him and her father turned towards them and her mother came from the kitchen to know what happened.

"What happened?" they both asked simultaneously.

"He is smart enough. I thought I had planned but he knew beforehand about all these." She said.

He was shocked. How can she tell all these to her parents? He was ashamed and felt guilty.

"Calm down, son. We wanted to meet you for which she planned all these. We are sorry. We did not mean to hurt you.", her father said.

"Please do not apologise, Sir. I did not mean to hurt you. Actually, I was wondering why she was acting although you all knew about it. I came here because I knew that you wanted to meet me but I did not know the purpose behind it."

"There is no such purpose. You are the only one she spoke about in last couple of months. She did not speak about anyone else and she said that you are lending your ears to her whenever she required, so we wanted to meet you. We are concerned about her and we wanted to know her pal who is having a great effect on her."

"I did not expect that though. I don't have any effect on anyone. She needed me some of the time and I had been with her whenever I was free. I believe that's what human beings are for, to help others when they are in need. Besides, there is an adage "a friend in need is a friend indeed.". I am trying to live up to my friendship and maintain this friendship as long as I can."

Her parents were taken aback by this guy. They appreciated their daughter's friend and his perception towards life. She had told them that his guts and wit were worth appreciation and that was what they found in him.

He was sad internally to find such a happy family and great parents. He felt how lucky Afsheen was to have such a great parents. He had fun with them, had dinner and left for his room.

"He is a nice guy, My Princess." her father told her in her mother's presence after he had left.

"Thank you, Dad."

"Do you like him?"

"He is a great friend of mine. I am glad that you had forecasted so and he really turned out to be exactly what you had told."

"I am still waiting for your answer. You know what I am asking."

"I like him, Dad, as a friend. Nothing beyond that and you know that I will tell you if anything ever happens like that."

"I know, sweetheart that you will tell us that. But remember that he is the perfect one for you and don't lose hope if he could not be with you as your hubby because he will always be with you. Besides, if he ever falls in love with someone, she would be the luckiest girl as he will love her more than himself and God knows what he will do if she leaves him at any given point of time."

"What do you mean, Dad?"

"His love is divine. He will never leave you because you see your best pal in him and he will live up to your expectations. He loves himself more than anyone else today and if he ever falls in love, he will love her more than his own self and if for any reason she leaves him then I do not know what his condition will be. I do not know what he will do. He will go insane may be. I just want you not to fall in love with him because if you fall in love with him and he didn't then you would be hurt and if he falls in love with someone else and was left alone then you won't get this guy ever. I am afraid about the consequences. I know that I am thinking far ahead which I should not but I am thinking about you, My Child. You will be the luckiest woman in this world if he ever falls in love with you. Never leave him as he will be there with you whenever you want him."

"Why are you saying so?"

"I can see myself in him. I know what my situation was when your Mom did not want to be with me because of her parents. I am afraid, My Sweetheart. I really am."

She came back from the school, switched on the TV and the news channel popped up. The breaking news showed "The flight to France was crashed and all the passengers died.". She could not believe her ears and eyes. She started searching for the information about the flight which was boarded by her parents.

He was on his way home and for some reasons, he decided to change his direction and went towards her home. He shared a strong telepathy with the people he was close to. While heading towards her home, his phone buzzed.

"Ya?", he asked.

She broke completely and cried. She could not utter a single word.

"Ashi, what happened? Why are you crying?"

She could reply nothing.

"Wait. I am on my way. Don't go anywhere. I will reach in five minutes."

He hung up the call and sped his bike.

The door was open. She was sitting on the floor, did not change her dress, bag was resting on the sofa and news channel was repeating the same thing over and over again.

He did not see the TV. He went to her, took her in his arms and she wailed holding him. He could not understand and there was no response from her when he asked her the reason.

"I won't stop you today like the other day. You cry as much as you want. I am here with you. But let me know the reason at least, Ashi." He said.

She said nothing and pointed her fingers towards the TV. He looked at the TV and fell apart. It did not take him much time to realise the situation. He went numb and cold.

He never had such a situation before and he did not know how to handle her. He switched off the TV and held her in his arms letting her cry. He did not try to console her even. The demise of her parents had left not only her in shock but him too. He cared and loved them as his parents too. He could not express his feelings as it would have affected Afsheen. He was broken inside but strong enough to take care of Afsheen.

The phone rang and he picked up.

"Hello?", he asked.

"How is Afsheen?", her maternal grandfather asked. They have known him too.

"She is good and won't be able to speak now."

"Okay. Do take care of her. We are reaching in a couple of minutes."

Her paternal grandparents turned up by the phone got disconnected. They were also weeping. Her eyes were blood red because of shedding tears since an hour. Her maternal grandparents also reached and they all were crying making it hard for him and Afsheen too. He did not know whom to speak to and what to do. He was blank and getting exasperated. He could not stand tears and there were so many people who were getting carried away without understanding the situation.

He asked both the grandpas to the corner of the hall.

"I don't know why you both are aggravating the situation rather than controlling it. I understand that you both have lost your son and daughter but Afsheen had lost her parents. If you both are going to weep then who will take care of her and your wives and family. I am not asking you to laugh in this situation but don't lose yourself. I know it is hard for you but you need to realise that you are making it harder for your family by shedding tears. If you both want to weep, then go to the washroom and weep. Then come back and start consoling them. I can't stand all these.", he said and started wailing like a kid.

He left that place without letting Afsheen know that he was crying. He returned back within a few minutes to them. Her grandpas had already taken control of the situation and he felt grateful to himself. They stayed there with her and she did not want him to leave. He stayed back too.

After the rituals, her grandparents wanted her to be with them but she turned them down. She wanted them to leave and asked him to be with her. He shifted to her place. He helped her with her daily chores, he stayed awake to ensure that she was sleeping peacefully. He would cook bread and omelette and sometimes some other dishes for her. She would deny and he would help her eat. Sometimes the food would be a complete mess and he would order from restaurants. He would admonish her whenever required. He became her parents and her best friend in the process.

They both went to school together after three weeks. She strictly asked her grandparents not to contact her and they called him up to know her situation. He would say that she is doing great and recovering and they would thank him. He was financially helped by them for their livelihood. He maintained the record of every penny given by them and every penny spent on day-to-day basis.

They were watching a movie on Saturday night when he said her to resume the school from Monday.

"I don't want to go to school." She replied.

"Okay, your wish. I won't say anything then, but I want to ask you one thing."

"Ya?"

"Do you think that you would drop from the school if they would have been here?"

"No.", she replied with a low voice.

"Then why are you doing this now? They are watching you, Ashi. They are with you, within you, around you. They can feel you and sense you. If you are doing something which you would not have done in their presence then you are hurting them. You are a beautiful and obliged daughter and they have always loved you. I just want you to make them proud. I want you to do the things which you would have done the way in their presence. I want you to live your life, it's your life. They had always wanted you to live your life. Isn't it?"

She did not reply anything.

"Ashi…. I am asking you something."

"Yes." She almost whispered.

"Then live. It's your life, baby. Don't spend it. Just live it. If you don't live your life the way you want then you will be forced to live your life the way life wants. Do you want to be forced by someone to do something?"

"No."

"Then live your life. Let's go to school. Let's start doing all those which you were doing."

"I need some more time."

"I don't want to give you any more time. I don't want you to focus on studies. I want you to go to school and be there. You don't need to speak to anyone if you don't feel like. Don't force yourself to do anything. Just go to school.

In fact, I will get a chance to travel in your luxurious cars in the process and some girls will start hitting on me for the reason."

She laughed. He looked at her with contentment in his heart. She had laughed for the first time in last three weeks. Her eyes filled with tears while laughing and she cried.

"Why did it happen? Why did they leave me?", she asked him.

"Do you believe in God?"

"Yes, I do." She replied.

"They say that God takes them to Him who are dearest to Him as there are only a few good people left with Him. That's why He took them."

"Don't you believe in God?" she asked.

"I believe in myself and they say God lies within self. I have never seen God and not sure I will ever see. I believe that there is a supreme power and people perceive that power in different forms. Most of them perceive in the form of God, Allah, Krishna, Buddha, etc. and I believe that power lies in the Universe, the nature. They are the Supreme Power for me. I believe in the power of nature."

"What would have you done if you would have been in my shoes?"

"First of all, I am in your shoes. They were not only your parents, they were mine too. I have always respected them as my parents. I have a responsibility now which they have left for me. The responsibility to take care of myself as well as yours. I am happy to have them in my life for a couple of years and you are a lucky girl, Ashi. And I am luckier because I have all of you in my life. They are within me, Ashi. They left me because they will come back to me in some other forms. People leave so that they can come back again. They will come back and don't ask me when and how because I don't have the answer to that."

"Hey, I want to thank you but I won't."

"Thank you for not thanking me. Shall we start our preparation for the school tomorrow?"

"Good night.", she said with a smile.

"Sweet night, Dear."

He covered her with the blanket, switched off the lights and sat on the couch.

"Why don't you sleep next to me?"

"No, it's fine. I just want to sit here for some time."

"Come and lie next to me."

He obeyed her.

She covered him with the same blanket and crossed her hand above him like a baby sleeps with its' parents, getting all their attention. He rested his head on one of his hands and she slept cuddling him.

He became her guide, her companion, her motivator, her coach and her best friend. He took care of her just like her parents did. He never complained, never exasperated. She spoke and he listened. He sometimes went cold and she kept mum. They built up a perfect chemistry of friendship. They were the best example of friendship. He laid his hands whenever she required and she stayed with him whenever he needed. She got addicted to him.

The years passed as if within minutes and the educational life came to an end and she was unsure of her career.

"I am not sure about my future.", she told him once while listening to the song "Message in a bottle" at her place.

"What interests you?"

"I always wanted to take care of my Dad's business for which I visited his office with Mom and Dad many a times before coming here. But I am not sure now."

"Go to France." His said with a stern voice.

"When shall we go?"

"Ashi, I am asking you to go. I am not coming with you."

"I am not going alone.", she confirmed.

"Don't be so adamant."

"I won't be able to do anything there. I don't know anyone. I don't know if the people who were there are still associated with us or not. I don't know what has happened over the past few years. Why don't you understand? I need you there."

"First of all, relax. Don't be so negative. I understand that you have concerns and we can sort out. I want you to think about all the possibilities and start working out. I don't want you to go today or tomorrow. I want you to get all the data, speak to people over there and then we will plan accordingly about your departure. Besides, I am always available for you over the phone and you know that. You can call me at any given point of time and I will be expecting a pay check for giving you suggestions because you will be a business woman then."

"Whatever I have, is yours. You do not need a pay check to receive my calls.", she laughed and he joined her.

They worked out on everything which was planned for her and the ticket was booked. The night before her departure she asked him to get some wine as she wanted to celebrate with him. He got a bottle of red wine and a bottle of white wine.

She opened the bottle of white wine first and served in two glasses.

"I want to reveal something before raising the toast so that you won't feel that I am drunk."

"What?"

"I love you, I really do. It's not because you are with me since a long time, you helped me with so many things or anything. I love you much before that."

"Do you remember what have I said you the very first day?"

"I do."

"Then don't love me. I will be there for you as long as I am alive as a friend and I don't want to spoil our relationship by getting married. I am really happy with our relationship. I am a self-absorbed egotist who can never love anyone more than self or care for, apart from self. I love myself the most, Ashi. You need to know that. I love you, I respect you too but as a human being, as a friend. Nothing lies beyond that. I am happy with this platonic relationship with you. I am really the luckiest fella in the world to have a person like you. The best part in our relationship is I can call you or barge in at the mid of the night even after your marriage without worrying what your husband will think. Don't get into this relationship. Let's raise the toast to our emotions and relationship."

They raised the toast and she kissed him on his cheek to show her love.

"Can you promise me something?"

"Promises are made to be broken, dear. Don't you know that?"

"Not for the beings like you."

"Shoot."

"I just want you to be with me forever and never leave me at any given point of my life."

"That's a weird stuff to promise. I promise that I will be with you as long as I can."

"That's the height of diplomacy."

"And you know what?"

"What?"

"If we get tied up then do you know how many hearts will break into pieces and how many will curse me, bombshell?"

They laughed a lot on this statement of his.

"Why do you make me laugh always even when I am serious?"

"I just want you to create things which will make you laugh. I want you to find reasons around you to bring a smile on your face irrespective of my presence or absence in your life. If you can make yourself laugh then no one can ever make you cry."

They slept next to each other and she cuddled him.

———◈———

Her phone buzzed the moment she switched it on after the flight landed at the airport.

"Hey."

"Hi. How are you?"

"I am great. I just switched it on and you called. I am with my bro now. Is it fine if I call you after reaching home?"

"How was the wedding?"

"It was great. We had lots of fun."

"Awesome. I am waiting for you at the arrival."

"You are kidding me."

"No. I am serious. Your parents are also there. See you soon. Bye."

"No, sweets. Don't be there."

"Bye, Saaya."

She came out and he was not there. She looked around for him but could not see him. She called him up to ensure that he was not there. He disconnected the call.

"I know that you would not have appreciated my presence there as your parents are already present. I am waiting for the day when you will introduce me to them. I left and you are looking terrific in this blue *salwar*." He texted.

"Sweets, I am sorry for this but you know my parents na and even my bro has also turned up. That's why.", she replied.

"Don't bother yourself. Send me a pic of yours in this dress. I want to treasure this. See you tomorrow. Have fun with your bro and parents. Tc"

She tried reaching him but there was no response. He did not care to call back even. He waited for her as usual but neither called her nor texted nor spoke to her. His silence made her insane. She could not bear his silence. It tortured her. Almost after a week, she came down to his place in the morning and when he opened the door, she hugged him and cried.

"Please speak to me, sweets. I can't bear your silence. It's freaking my mind out. Please don't be so harsh on me. Please try to understand. You don't know my parents. I know how they are. Please, sweets."

"I am sorry. I did not mean to hurt you. I believe you deserve someone from your community as you could not say to your parents about us and you don't want me to speak to them even."

"I am feeling so relaxed after listening to you.", she said while hugging him and kissed him. She continued, "They are looking out for guys. I don't want to meet them. I don't want to see any guy. I want to see you only. I was tensed when I heard this. My mother was having so many expectations. She wants a guy from a good family with a good package, with cooks and maids so that I won't have to do anything so that I will live my life like a queen. My father wants someone having their own home and the guy to be educated. I can't make them understand about us. I want you to be self-sufficient so that you can come and speak to them. I can linger it for two years, not more than that. You have to prove yourself within these two years and speak to them so that they won't have any reason to turn you down."

"Would you be with me when I come and speak to them?"

"Sweets, prove yourself and make yourself sufficient."

"Saaya, I am going to France."

"What? Why? When?"

"I will join Ashi. I have not spoken to her yet but I will speak to her and leave for France soon. I believe it will resolve our self-sufficiency part."

"You do whatever you want to. I want you to earn enough so that it won't be the criteria for disqualifying you.'

"Let me see what I can do. I need you and it's impossible for me to live without you. You need to understand that."

"Hey, Ashi."

"Hi. I reached an hour ago."

"Good. How is everything out there?"

"Awesome. What happened? You are disturbed."

"Well, do you have any opportunity for me out there?"

"Are you freaking serious?"

"Yes, I am."

"How did the mind change, Mr.?"

"Well, you know I am not satisfied with my job or package. I hope you can help me out with that."

"What's the matter, dear?"

"Saaya."

"Okay. I got it. When are you planning to come?"

"Next week."

"I will take care of your arrangements. Give me a day and thank Saaya on my behalf."

"For what?"

"Finally, you are coming to be with me. I don't care whatever the reason is but you are coming and that's enough for me."

"Let me know the requirement and I will email you."

"Sure. Don't stress yourself. I am just a call away. Take care, Dumbo."

"You too."

S he called him to wait for her at the bus stop a bit early as she wanted to go out with him. He reached there and she did not keep him awaited for long this time.

"Hi. Where shall we head to?", he asked.

"I wanted to go to the beach."

They took a cab and went to the beach. It was looking great at the dawn. The sun was setting, couples were busy displaying their affection in front of the public and the hawkers were yelling.

They held each other's hand and their shoes in the other.

"I hate this PDA. And you never try to do that."

"Okay. But what this PDA is?"

"Public Display of Affection. It seems so weird. I don't understand why they are so desperate." She replied.

"Okay. Something new to learn. I am flying next week."

"When?

"I don't know. Ashi will send all the details tomorrow."

"You know what?"

"Hmm?"

"I feel jealous of her. I know that I should not but still."

"I understand but you don't need to feel jealous. I am in safe hands and I can assure you that. I wanted you to meet her but it could not happen. Anyways"

"I wanted to tell you something."

"Hmm?"

"I love you, sweets and my parents are after my life to get me married. I am saved because of my father. I want you to turn every stone to make this happen."

"Hmm."

"There was a guy in that marriage who is tall and fair and earning a handsome amount. One of my relatives spoke to my mother about him and my mother is taking that relative seriously. She thinks I am getting too old and I should get married ASAP. I denied her."

"Why don't you speak to her about us?"

"I spoke to her indirectly. I told her what if I marry someone from other caste. She got furious and then said '*if you want me to die then tell me, I will die. I don't want to be beaten to death by your father*'. And she ensured that I am not into any relationship and I had just asked her gently. I can't keep lying to them, sweets. It hurts me. I can't hurt them."

"Do you want to leave me? Do you want to go ahead?"

"You know that I can't leave you and even I can't betray them."

"Don't worry everything will be fine."

"I just want to tell you one incident which I heard in the function."

"Hmm?"

"We had a common friend who fell in love with a guy from north. Her parents never liked him. They eloped. They got married in a temple. She got pregnant and he asked her to abort. She denied and he warned her that he would leave her if she did not abort. She aborted. After that he left her. She did not have any proof to show that they were married. There had no photos of the marriage, the marriage was not registered even. Finally, she got the abortion letter where he had signed as her husband. That guy was jailed and the girl returned to her parents. They arranged a guy for her who was working abroad and this girl revealed her past to him before marriage although her parents had asked her not to divulge this. She disclosed everything to ensure that the guy's life is not ruined in future. The guy thanked her for being so open and telling the truth. He accepted her and married her. The very day after her marriage he took her along with him rather than leaving her at his place."

"Wow…. that's awesome. Love, betrayal, trust and truth are the summary. Initially, she was betrayed by the one whom she had believed that she loved however he loved her body not her soul and later she found her soul mate. I salute that guy who accepted her after knowing everything and that girl who had the guts to keep her past in front of him. They both will live happily forever just because their relationship was based upon truth, trust and transparency. Do you trust me?"

"Sorry?" she thought he did not ask and that rather was a statement.

"Do you trust me?"

"Yes, I do. I don't want to know why you asked this."

"You just need to know that I love you more than yesterday and less than tomorrow." His voice was low and an air of melancholy had surrounded his heart which she could sense.

"I love you too, sweets.", she confessed while pressing his hands.

"Don't ever leave me. I know that I fight with you, I shout at you which you don't like, I become frigid at times but remember that I love you rather than all these. I would fight with you in the morning and pamper you at night. I would love to have a baby girl from you. I would prefer to sleep in your arms at night and plant a good night and good morning kiss. I would prefer to listen to your whole day's story and bug you with my balderdash speech. I would bore you but make our life interesting and adventurous. I would like to travel the whole world with you. I would do whatever I can to make you happy and in return I expect something."

"Expectation is the worst thing in this world and still we expect as these are the by-products of the relationships. I am surprised to find that you are having expectations from me. I have never seen you expecting anything from anyone but your own self. I would love to live up to your expectations."

"I would expect you to understand me when I am cold rather than having any offence and never leave me irrespective of anything. I know it's not easy but still." He pleaded.

"*Je t'aime*, Sweets.", she said and he flew to France two days after.

He was born in a higher middle class family to a corrupted father and a gloated mother. His father was a government employee who made a fortune by taking bribe and never spoke evil about anyone. He worked really hard to reach the highest position in his work. He never asked anyone to pay him and when someone paid him, he demanded more as if it was his right. He spent the whole evening with his family. He never boozed or smoked or chewed. He was an idol for the people who came in his contacts because of his way of getting connected to people.

His mother was not only a virago but also a licentious. She had many affairs in her life, what they say was extra-marital affair. His parents had a devastated family life. They fought every now and then. There was no peace ever in that house. Peace lies within and peace stays in a home but there was no within, it's only without, without peace. There was no home. Home needs to be the safest and quietest place in this world and you find the eternal peace or abysmal love when you step in as if all the exhaustion vanished and you are all relieved. But this was not a home, not even a house. It was a place surrounded with four walls where people during the day came to have a physical contact and verbal contact in the evening.

They say time heals everything, probably not. He witnessed his mother's lecherous activities with many people over the period and he thought he could direct a porn movie. He supported neither of his parents when they abused each other verbally. He would either increase the volume of the music or leave that place which they called as a house or home and spend hours outside. Sometimes he did not care to return till midnight. He lived a life of isolation in the world of tiffs.

He was afraid of darkness and his life made darkness his best friend. He was good at studies and everyone in his family had a hope that he would cross all the milestones in his life and print his name on the hearts of many people. That he would set an example for others in terms of career. He did set an example not for others but for himself. His maturity level was of a forty years at the age of ten. He was sharp-minded and loved to be alone in his own world of thoughts. He was accepted by his friends in the school for his comradeship. He was great at changing topics and avoiding stuffs which he did not like. He was straight-forward with a sugar coated voice.

His parents loved him and he loved both of them more than himself until the day he overheard the tiff between his parents.

"Why the hell did you sleep with me to get me pregnant and let this guy take birth?", his mother had asked.

"What's the guarantee that my blood is running in him?", his father had been blunt with his reply.

He had locked his room and cried the whole night, slept throughout the day and missed his classes for a couple of days for the first time in his life. He was traumatized. No one from his voice could recognize his emotional state but his face and eyes said everything. He knew how to avoid questions and he tackled them in a polished manner. He was trying to convalescence but he could not help himself. He was getting more into those thoughts. He knew that his emotions were about to explode in near future either in the form of anger or tears or silence or terror. He did not know in which form it would explode but he knew that it would and he would be left alone post explosion. He was contented with the feeling of being alone.

Finally on his day of birth, he decided to take his life. He was hospitalised and recovered at a faster rate as he wanted to live. That was when he had seen death in front of him. He had realised that

"Death is beautiful, it's the awesome thing which can ever come across someone's life but life is beautiful, it's seriously beautiful than death. If you live every moment without a pinch of angst, worry, trauma, hatred and a feeling of revenge, you will see what life has to offer you."

He decided to live and he did everything to fight against the venom within him to get back to his life. His parents cried and prayed for his life but he did not have any more respect or love for them. The venom had killed the respect and love within him for them. The doctors, the nurses and the trainees spent time with him to find out the reason for that decision of his. They could not believe that a guy who was smiling at his death bed and fighting to live could take such a step. No one knew the reason behind his action but he.

So many people said so many things. Many conclusions were reached as a reason of his action but he cared for any. He was giving his best to live. He had perceived by then that life was his and he would be carefree and selfless to live his life. He had changed his way of life during those days. He had imagined how his life would be. He knew that he would fall in love with the only person who would respect him, adore him, care for him and take his responsibility and that person was none other than himself. He knew that they would call him selfish instead of selfless and careless instead of carefree but he was least bothered. He was least concerned about the world now. He was ready to use everyone but himself. He would remain true to his soul, his eternal self and never-ending thoughts.

The doctor discharged him and he left for those four walls. He had no more emotions for anyone and he was finally contented to come back to his life but fate had decided something else for him. After getting discharged, he had a nervous breakdown and he went under treatment. People were scared of him and literally afraid to approach him or speak to him. He did whatever he wanted to and left out frequently even during the medication. He met frequent accidents and never bothered to worry about the pain or the blood. He knew that he would recover from the pain borne by his muscles but the pain borne by his heart can never be recuperated. The scratches on his body would leave a scar which would be forgotten by his grey cells but the scar in his grey cells could never be recouped.

He fought with his internal self to come out of all those. He had started a cold war with his fate and decided that he would never let his fate win. He did win to prove himself, and that he was worth being a human. If the world was full of human beings then he considered himself a barbarian.

He went to school while recovering and suss out that there were lots of rumours and truth lies nowhere around. He laughed and no one understood the reason behind his laughs. Many called him insane and some came close to him to find out the reason. He always kept space for himself. He had only a few close friends and he made everyone felt that each one was his closest buddy. No one ever knew what's running in his mind and moreover, no one bothered to know. And within a week, everyone forgot about the rumours.

He developed an interest for girls to fill the hole inside his soul and became close to girls. He had never allowed them to come too close to him but he penetrated their minds. Girls came and left in his life and no one stayed with him for more than a few months but one. He left her after a few months saying her that she was not worth him. He could never see the light on anyone which matched the light on him. He got infatuated to everyone where the light within him sparked for someone. He could never find the light within him getting completely immersed in the other side to find the radiance which would burn both the souls to make one. He spoke in the same way with the opposite sex the way he spoke to the same gender.

There was a girl who was hitting on him for a week and he did not give a glance at her and later on she had said a classmate of his that she had never seen someone with such attitude. Girls are so delicate. If you don't speak to them then you have an attitude and if you do then they think as if you are hitting on them. He was no more interested in what people said. He had become self-centric and when a senior told him that he was egoistic in front of his class, he went to him, looked at his face and replied,

"I know what I am. If you have to say something about me then say something which I am not aware of about myself. Don't waste your time and mine by saying something which I know about myself. I didn't lose my temper because I know that you are irritated and have revealed something which was a complete wastage of your energy. If I tell you something about yourself then you would lose your temper as you don't know yourself the way I know myself.", and he had continued, "Do you know what?"

"What?", he asked vehemently.

"Sometimes the middle finger speaks more than the words." he had a smile when he blurted.

The whole class could not stop laughing with his last statement. The guys laughed and the girls giggled while the senior left lowering his head.

He stayed calm and did not discuss about it later. While his classmates entertained themselves with that encounter and asked him again and again though he never repeated.

Afsheen had joined lately and they had exchanged a brief introduction on the very first day and they did not speak to each other post that. There were only two students who were hushed after his confrontation with his senior. One Afsheen, who was surprised and disturbed with this guy's attitude towards life and other human beings and the second one, he, himself, who was completely silenced and lost in a different world as if he was trying to calm down the volcano which had erupted before sometime.

Afsheen had wanted to speak to him after that incident but he had never entertained her. He had spent most of the time at his friends' place after leaving hospital and later shifted to Afsheen's place after her parents' demise.

His parents initially had been against this as she was a girl and the primary reason she being a Muslim but he had not listened to them. They listened to their relatives and whenever they discussed about these, he replied that they were their relatives not his and thus they never said him anything later. When she had asked him about his parents, he had replied that he needed her more than them. She knew that she needed him and he did not need her since he never needed anyone in his life.

He became more polite and responsible after shifting to her place. He became more carefree in his attitude and stopped using the sugar coated words and sentences. He felt that life was meant to live with self and not anyone else. He also understood the fact one should help everyone whenever there is a chance since he helped himself during his bad times. Most of the people do not know how to help themselves. So, he helped them to make them understand to help self. He never expected anything in return from them, neither good nor bad. He had no expectations from anyone but self.

He had looked out for jobs and tried different types of jobs since his school days to be independent. After his studies, he started his career with a small firm in accounts section for a mere which he had later left due to work pressure and less compensation. He had joined the BPO sector where he worked for a couple of months and then left because he did not enjoy the profile. He had thanked himself for joining the BPO as it had taught him how to communicate with people either over the voice or through vocabularies. Later, he had joined a local garment company to sell its' products. He enjoyed it for which he joined an IT company as sales executive.

That's the place where he met Sayuri, his Saaya. He saw her for the first time at the bus stop. The lights within him got attracted towards the invisible light within her. He thought it to be an infatuation and he did not want to get involved in any further relationship. He was fed up with all these and wanted to enjoy his life without any more girls. He saw her everyday but never spoke to her. Sometimes their eyes met and sometimes their hands brushed against each other. He never looked at her deliberately or waited intentionally. Months passed without the exchange of a single word. One summer evening, she was rushing to catch the bus but she missed. She started to breathe heavily and sat down to get hold of her breathe. She opened her bag to look out for her bottle of water. She took the bottle of water and found the bottle empty.

"Damn.", she said with exasperation. It seemed as if she forgot to fill her bottle in a hurry to leave office or catch the bus or reach her destination.

He had been observing her since the moment she had come. He handed over his bottle of water to her and she denied.

"It's fine.", she said.

He opened the bottle of water, drank some and then asked, "Are you sure?"

"No.", she took the bottle of water and said, "Thanks." with a smile and emptied the bottle.

"The pleasure was all mine, madam.", he replied.

"So?", she asked.

"Nothing." He replied and did not speak to her and looked for the bus.

He did not speak to her since then and he never acknowledged her greetings. She was offended with his arrogance. He was afraid to get into a relationship and he refrained himself completely.

It was raining heavily one day and he did not carry his raincoat or umbrella and she was standing under the umbrella. She looked at him and asked him to take shelter under her umbrella. He followed her instruction without uttering a single word.

"Why don't you speak to me?" she asked.

"Thank you."

"What?" she asked with a surprise.

"Thanks for giving me shelter under your umbrella."

Her face was wet and some of hair too, which covered her side face. It seemed as if she had just come out of the shower. She looked awesome. She was wearing a long black skirt and a red tops.

"You are looking great today." She complimented him.

"Was it a compliment or sarcasm?", he asked as if she read his mind.

"You have your own thoughts. You believe what you want to believe. If I explain it to you then it will be in vain as the mind perceives what it wants to rather than thousands of explanations."

"Then I will take it as a compliment."

They exchanged each other's numbers and stayed in touch. They chatted, in general, whenever they were free and left together for their homes in the evening. Most of the time, he waited for her in the evening. She told him about her family, her family's expectations, her dream to become the VP of a company in next 15 years and her hobbies. He listened to her and he blabbered most of the time. He spoke to her about his office, his frustration, his lack of satisfaction in his job and so on.

He had left the IT Company where he was working after finding a job in a FMCG company in the near-by area so that they could meet every day and come home together. He had shifted to a place close to her home so that he could accompany her. He enjoyed her company and refrained himself from letting her being close to him or vice-versa.

They were neither friends nor colleagues nor did they have any relationship. They were just strangers who spoke to each other while travelling to kill their time or enjoy the companionship. They discussed about various topics from sports to politics to archaeology to history to finance and what not. Sometimes, he would just listen to her and stare at her like an ignorant person as if he did not have any knowledge about the topic which she brought up. She used to study his body language and facial expression to confirm that he was unaware of the topic and then she would make him understand in detail and he would behave like an obedient and curious student by intervening her with some questions. She would answer all his questions patiently.

They were two different chemicals which would have created a great chemical reaction if combined but they were repelling each other. They needed a catalyst to form a great reaction. They even did not know that they needed a catalyst. He deliberately refrained from her and she had her obligation towards her parents.

They did not know that something out there was observing them, more closely than the air, something which was keeping an eye on them and wanting them to break all the reasons and come close to each other. It was nothing but the destiny. Destiny had decided something for them which they were unaware of. No one could ever mess with it and it has got all the rights to mess with anyone without letting them know. It can either make or break anyone or anything as per its' wish. What a dreadful and unpredictable thing it is. Some fear it and some laugh at it but it remained stoic laughing back at them.

"Hey, Sweets.", she said in a whispering note, which she generally did while speaking to him at night so that she would not be caught by someone at home.

"Hi, Saaya. I love this voice of yours." He admired her voice as he always did. He loved her voice when she was either half-asleep or got up from her sleep. He could do anything to listen to that voice of hers and feel her breathe.

"When did you reach?"

"The flight just landed and I called you up."

She said something which he could not listen.

"I am unable to hear you properly as you are speaking slowly. Is it fine if I call you once I reach the room?"

"Hmm. Bye."

He checked out, collected his luggage and walked towards the exit as if he had been there earlier and the place was known to him. It actually was known to him as Afsheen had told him many times while checking out. She was waiting for him and waived at him when he reached the exit door. And she hugged him tight when he reached her.

"How was the trip, Dumbo?"

"Fantastic. And thank you."

"For what?"

"For waiting for me, for riding me to your home, letting me come here and moreover, being with me since so many years."

"What's wrong? Is everything fine?"

"Nothing is wrong and everything is fine. In short, I was missing you, and happy to see you after long."

"I too missed you", she responded back while holding him tightly. Her eyes were full of tears.

"Who are you dating?"

"Ahh…. None. You know that I will never do that. I will start dating as you are here now."

"Stop flirting, Ashi. I will live with you and fulfil all your wishes but I won't be dating you."

"Don't. When did I ask you to date me? I said I will date you." she burst out laughing.

The following day he reached her office and she introduced him to everyone around. He pointed out the things which he did not like and asked her to leave him for a couple of hours to go through the files of accounts.

After a few hours, they went to an Indian restaurant near-by.

"I would like to know about your plans post-lunch."

"Do you mean to say about my marriage, I mean our marriage? No, not now", she giggled.

"Jokes apart, Ashi. I am serious. I want to know about your plans and your thoughts for the company.

"Nothing to hurry, Idiot. We have enough time to discuss about all these. You have reached here yesterday and I had some plans for this evening. No more work for the day. Alright?"

"No, it's not. I am here so that you can get the best out of me and exploit me completely as the MNCs do."

"I will exploit you, dear. Don't you worry about it. I will exploit you in my own way. Got it?"

"Yes, Ma'am."

His phone buzzed and he disconnected the call and called back.

"Hey, Sweets. I am sorry I slept off last night while speaking to you. I did not realise when I slept."

"I know. I was listening to your breathe. Thank you. How is the day going?"

"Good. What are you up to?"

"Nothing much. We are having lunch now. I will tell you how the taste was once we finish it up. It's an Indian restaurant."

"Okay. How was your journey and how is everything going on?"

"Superb. The only thing is I am missing you. I feel like hugging you tightly."

"Stop flirting and have lunch properly. I will call you when I leave office. My boss is sitting on my head."

"I understand. You take care of yourself. I will wait for your call."

"Lucky Saaya.", Afsheen said when he dropped the call.

"I am lucky to have both of you in my life and you are the luckiest to have me in your life.", he mimicked.

She drove him to Marineland after lunch.

"Wow!", he exclaimed.

"It's my favourite place. Whenever I think of you or Dad or Mom, I come here. I spend some time with myself thinking about all the beautiful moments which I have lived with all of you, enjoy the serenity and then leave. Most of the time I called you up when I was here."

"Why are you being so emotional?"

"Because you are there with me to take care of my emotions."

"I can take care of your emotions but I can't take care of your car as I neither know the left hand driving nor do I have a driver's license of this country."

She laughed and he felt contented.

They enjoyed the tranquillity of the natural aura and spent some time with the dolphins before leaving. They enjoyed their silence and spoke their mind without speaking a single word while returning.

He did whatever he could to develop the process and get more business. She gave him all the liberty. He went with the sales personnel to visit the client and crack the order right away. He worked closely with the finance, procurement, human resource and administration to get the best out of everything. He was a fast learner and never gave up on anything. He admitted whenever he did not know something and sought the help of his colleagues to know about it. He brought a change in her organisation or rather his organisation. He asked everyone to leave their respective desk on Friday an hour before and had get-together over high-tea. He ensured work over the weekends on not even work from home. He strictly mentioned not to discuss about work. The employees from different departments and started knowing each other from and started knowing each other personally. Two months later, Afsheen was shocked to discover that the effectiveness of the employees had increased. Sometimes, he even conducted self-motivating session for the employees. They were passionate looking at his enthusiasm.

He and Afsheen worked late during the weekdays and went for long drive or visited different places over the weekends. He was enjoying this to the core and never missed a call of his Saaya. If he was busy then he would receive the call and tell her that he would call her back as he was in the midst of something. She was happy knowing about his performance. He gave as much time as he could to Sayuri and the whole time was for Afsheen after leaving office till they slept. Even if the phone did not show the name of Saaya, his mind would anyway be lost in her thoughts.

It seemed completely perfect to him. He thought he would bring Sayuri to her dream land and settle down there which would fulfil all his needs and her dreams. Whenever he spoke to Sayuri, he would be full of energy. She found him unwearied and she was happy for him, for her, for them.

Afsheen was highly religious and she always took time out for her prayers and celebrated all the festivals. He went on fast with her during Ramzaan and she enjoyed Diwali and Holi with him. She called up her grandparents every day at least for a minute.

"Hey, Dumbo?", she called him.

"Hmm?"

"I did not see you calling your parents in last 6-7 months. What's wrong? You never revealed to me about your family members. You know my story and I am an open book for you."

He looked at her, gave a sarcastic smile and replied, "I had read this statement somewhere a long time back which I would love to share with you *'I was born and raised by those who praise control of population.'*" he continued without having an eye contact with her, "I have nothing to share or reveal. I am what I am. How does it matter what my parents were or are, how does it matter what my life was or is, how does it matter what the past was when my present is awesome with the two most beautiful girls of this world and my future is going to be mind-blowing? Ashi, I don't know what's wrong, because I never wanted to know. I know that you are a part of my life and Saaya is another part and that's enough for me. I can live without you but I will always be there for you. I know that you always will be there beside me irrespective of whether I want you or not, but it's not possible for me to live without Saaya. I love both of you and would appreciate to be with you two forever. I would be the luckiest fella of your God's creation if I get a chance to have both of your physical presence and her love and soul with me till my last beat.", his voice choked and he stopped.

"I didn't know that you love her so much.", she said while handing over a glass of water to him.

"People believe that I respect all of them just because of the way I behave with them but the fact is I respect only three people in this world and no one else."

He paused and she did not ask him to reveal as she thought he would say and he was expecting her to ask.

"Who are they?" finally she asked.

"I respect myself and you two beautiful lasses of my life and this universe. Thank you for giving me your heart and mind and thanks to her for giving me her soul."

She hugged him and did not let him speak anything else. She knew that if he uttered a single word then she would break into tears and her love for him would hurt him and he was already in a state of desolation.

<hr>

"Hey, Sweets. How are you?", she asked.

"I am great. I am booking tickets for you to come down to your dream land."

She laughed mockingly, "You know that I can't."

"It's being unbearable for me. I need to see you. I can't wait and I can't come. Please come. I will book the tickets for you and we will have fun." He was desperate in his voice.

"You know, Hottie, that I can't come. You know my parents na."

"I am settled now and you need to speak to them about us now. I had told you not to reveal them about us earlier as I was not stable but I want you to tell them now."

"No, I can't. You don't know how they are. And they are after my life to get married now. My father was not discussing about this earlier but he has also started talking about my marriage now. I am tensed. My mother is getting proposals for me and they want me to go and meet guys. I don't want to meet anyone apart from you."

"Then speak to them about us."

"I can't."

"Then start meeting guys and move on. You are neither letting me speak to them nor are you speaking to them. I understand their expectations and I am settled now."

"Let me see."

"There is nothing to see. I just want you to close this topic. Either you speak to them or start meeting guys and move on.", his voice was rude and he was losing his temper.

"You know na, Sweets, that I can't move without you. I never passed time with you. I was always serious about you. I am never going to leave you. Just remember that. I will never let you go and flirt with other girls. I will always keep an eye on you and never let you leave me.", she said with a lighter note.

"Saaya,", his voice low, "I can't live without you. I will tell you thousands of times to leave me and go ahead just because you love your parents so much but I will definitely not want you to leave me, ever. Let's find some way out. Okay?"

"Okay".

"I will call you back. I have some work. I am missing you more than yesterday and less than tomorrow."

"And I love you more than yesterday and definitely less than tomorrow."

He went to Afsheen's chamber and closed the door behind him.

"What happened, Idiot?" she asked.

"Ashi, I have to go back for a couple of days."

"Is there any problem?"

"Nothing, Dear. It's her birthday. I wanted her to come here but she turned me down. You know about her parents. I want to be with her on her birthday and will return within a week."

She called up the admin department and asked them to book the ticket for him.

He did not ask her to accompany him nor did she propose.

He took the flight, booked a room in the hotel near to her office and waited at the bus stop for her. He did not tell her about his arrival. He had planned this surprise for her. She tried reaching him the previous night but his number was switched off. She was irate and did not want to speak to him. She wanted to speak to him the whole night and her plans were ruined. He called her up in the morning and she did not reply. He texted her and there was no reply.

She got down from the bus and walked towards her office. He walked slowly behind her without letting her know. When she reached the gate of her office, he said.

"Excuse me, Madam. Can I gift you this bouquet and this French perfume on your birthday?"

She turned at him, looked with disbelief, hugged him and kissed him in front of everyone.

"Happy birthday, Saaya. I am sorry I could not call you last night as I was in the flight."

"I was waiting for your call the whole night and I was really hurt."

"Sorry, birthday girl."

"Shall you bunk the office today as you have never bunked your classes during school days?"

"Na. I can't. You know how my boss is and I have loads of work."

"Will you ever say "yes" on the first time?"

"No"., she said and giggled.

"I am waiting for you here. Come as soon as you can."

"I will come by 1 o' clock."

"I am waiting for you. You are great at keeping me awaited. Don't worry, I still will wait for you."

He waited for her almost two hours to come back. She again hugged him.

"I missed you so much and I am still missing you although you are just in front of me." He said.

"Hmm…. What's the plan, Sweets?"

"It's your day, Ma'am. You plan. I am all yours for as long as you want."

"You are always going to be mine. I will never leave you. I will not get married as I don't want anyone else apart from you, Hottie."

"Hmm. I am famished. Where shall we head to?"

They went to the same restaurant where they had been to have sizzlers and went for a movie after lunch. She had received some calls which she ignored. They went to the beach where they found couples everywhere either busy kissing or hugging each other.

"It seems so weird." He exclaimed.

"No PDA, Sweets." she said when he wanted to get close to her.

"I just want to cross your fingers with mine. Nothing more and it's not PDA."

"When are you returning?"

"Whenever you want me to."

"I don't want you to go. I just want you to stay back. My parents are serious about my marriage and I don't want you to go unless we are married."

"Done. Your wish is my command. I am staying back."

"What will you do?"

"You don't need to worry about it. It will be taken care of."

He dropped her at her place and went to the broker who had helped him to get the flat almost a year ago.

"I need that flat.", he said to the broker.

"That flat is already occupied. I can show you better ones."

"I need that one. Let me know the possible ways. Everything will be taken care of."

"Give me a day's time. I will get back to you by tomorrow afternoon." He replied when he heard about the commission part. He understood that he will be paid comparatively much more.

"Don't delay and I need it ASAP as it was then." he said and left.

The following day the broker called him and said that it would cost half a lakh apart from the security and brokerage. He agreed and asked him to paint the rooms in white.

After a week, he moved to the room which was filled with her memories, where she had come for the very first time, where they had their first kiss but the only change was the colour of the room. It was white then which was her favourite colour. She always wanted to have a white home and there it was. He was so excited. She came the day he shifted and was surprised to find it to be in white.

"For you, my Angel."

"Thank you." And she hugged him and kissed him for long.

"You will get all the furniture this time. It will be a home now, it won't be just a flat anymore."

"Sweets, I am really worried. I am going to meet a guy's parents tomorrow. I really don't want to meet them."

"When can we speak to your parents?"

"Sweets, why don't you understand? You don't know them. They have their own expectations. My mother is looking out for a guy from the same community. I can't make them understand. I spoke to my mother many a times indirectly and every time she broke into tears."

"Let me go and speak to them."

"No. Please don't.", she requested.

"I won't tell anything then. You do whatever you want to. You move on with whoever they want to. If you want to move on, then just leave me and go ahead with whomever they are finalising." He said with disgust in his voice and a pitch of anger in his tone.

They lay next to each other and he did not say anything.

———◆———

"How was the meeting?", he asked her the following day in the afternoon. He had not called her up since she had left the day before.

"It was good. They were really down to earth and my parents liked them a lot."

"What about the guy?"

"He was not there. He stays abroad."

"Did you like them?"

"They are simple and kind."

"Cool."

He called her up and texted her as usual and found to be ignored. He thought she must have been angry with him because of the last fight. He did not take it much to his heart and bought a king size bed with a snow white mattress, a cupboard, a dining table, a television initially.

The number of calls and messages had dropped and he thought it's just another tiff like the past.

"How is everything going on?", he asked one day when she was returning from her office.

"Good."

"How about the marriage stuff?", he asked to pull her legs.

"I will tell you once everything is finalised. The guy's parents had turned up with their relatives to our home and my parents had been to his place."

"It's moving then. Good.", he said with a mocking voice and he disconnected the call before his voice could choke.

He was sure that she would get back to him and she was doing all these because of her parents. Destiny, such an astonishing and amazing thing. It had decided their fate. It had decided earlier to bring them closer and after bringing them like the two sides of a coin, it had decided to separate both the sides. It had decided to take the grey cells out of the brain or the blood out of the cells. It had decided to block the paths of veins and arteries to heart.

She started avoiding his calls and texts and once texted him

"I am keeping distance from you."

He felt bad after reading the message. Time passed by and she grew into his thoughts more and more. He finally decided to speak to her and ask her to come back as he was nothing without her and he could not control himself. His life had become like a hollow trunk.

He went to the bus stop where he had not been to since a long time. She came and forced a smile on her face when her eyes finally caught by his.

"Hi. How are you?", he asked.

"I am good. How are you?" the voice was straight without any emotions and there were no more Sweets or Hotties.

"You seem so. How is everything going on?"

"Good.", it seemed as if she was not interested to speak to him at all.

"Would you like to say something?"

"Would you like to come to my wedding?"

He was taken aback by her question. His mind went blank and his heart stopped beating. He could not stop his tear glands and his body went numb while his breathe were interrupted by the void.

"When is it?"

"In December, after eight months. We have booked the hall also."

He did not know what to say, how to communicate, his body went cold and his throat choked. He felt as if his soul would free his body right away. He thought she would be interrogated by the public if anything happened to him. He managed to get some water. He took control over his body and mind. He gathered all his grey cells to one point.

"Saaya, I could not live without you. Please don't do this."

"Listen, I have decided to move on and I am moving on. Nothing is going to change my decision."

"You had even decided that you will never leave me."

"I have someone in my life now and his family too. I would appreciate not to dig into my past."

"Wow…. I have become your past. It took you only two months to bury your eight years. That's incredible. Listen Saaya, I can't leave you or live without you. I will speak to your parents or else let's elope. Please try to understand that I can't live without you. I love you, dammit. I never passed time with you. It has always been a serious relationship between us."

"I love him and I am marrying him. My parents are really happy and no one has any rights to hurt them. No one, I mean. It's my life, let me live the way I want. You had asked me to move on. Why are you doing all these when I am finally moving on?"

He was speechless. He was nervous. He had no answers. His thoughts were tied. He was in a world of nowhere. He fell down, his body was frozen and tongue dried. He could not move his fingers or hands. She thought he was acting. She did not care and left him. It took him almost an hour to recover.

Afsheen had called him up when he was alone and he did not remember what he had spoken to her. He managed to reach his room. He took his phone out to see if he had missed any calls or received any texts from her and there were seven calls from Afsheen.

He typed, "Thanks for not caring for me anymore and leaving me in the mid of nowhere." and pressed on "Send".

"I care for you and I know that you would not believe if I say so. Don't contact me henceforth and don't stop writing. Good bye."

"je t'aime more than yesterday and less than tomorrow. Do take care of my shadow. Take care." He replied.

Afsheen cancelled all her meetings, booked the ticket and reached him the following day. She directly came to his flat and rang the doorbell. There was no response. She knocked the door and still there was no response. He opened the door after ten minutes and she got in.

"Sorry, I was sleeping.", his eyes were blood red as he had been crying, he had no energy as he had not eaten anything since a few days.

"What happened?"

"Nothing." He said and cried holding her.

He had never cried in front of her and that day he was cried like a child. He rested his head on her lap and cried for hours.

"Would you say what's going on, dear?" she asked her with a soft tone.

Still there was no response.

"When is she getting married?"

"December."

She did not ask him anything and neither did he leave her the whole night. He slept on her lap and she remained awake, thinking about him, his conversation with her when he was, with her, in France.

When he got up in the morning, he was surprised to find himself on her lap. He remembered nothing since last morning.

"When did you come?", he asked her.

"When you needed me."

"Did you have anything?"

"Neither did you. Let's have something.", she took the menu card placed in the drawer and ordered for them.

"I need a help."

"Say."

"I will tell you when the time comes."

"I am waiting for that time desperately."

"How is the business running?"

"Everyone is missing you there."

"Tell them to remember all the moments which we had shared. Missing someone is the worst thing."

"That's what you did when you were there and that's what you are doing here."

"You are not speaking to her." He said.

"Definitely not."

"You are never going to blame her just like these human beings."

"I have got no reasons to blame her. I want you to come with me."

"I won't be able to."

"Don't say that you won't be able to, just say that you don't want to."

"That's what if you say."

"I need you, Dumbo. Why don't you understand that?"

"Can you promise me to do something for me?"

"Sure. You know that I don't even need to promise you to do something for you.", she assured.

"I want you to love yourself than anyone else."

"That's what you were doing when we met in school."

"I want you to take care of yourself so that you can take care of the business, the employees and everything related to you.", he demanded.

"You were the one who had told me that I could never take care of anyone until and unless I take care of myself."

"Can't you just stop replying and listen to me?"

"I don't want to."

"I have become a hypocrite. I have finally become a bloody human being, Ashi."

He asked her to leave and look after her business. She left by ensuring that he would respond to her calls whenever she called him up and he would speak to her every day. She did not want to leave him but she had to.

He did not speak to anyone but her whenever she called him. There was no sign of his Saaya. She did not call him and he did not want to intervene in her life as he knew that she was happy looking at the smile on his parents' face.

He hid himself in his room in complete darkness. He never switched on the lights and the fan was switched on twenty-four hours along with the music. He ate whenever he was hungry and drank water to wet his mouth. He did not know how many days had passed when he finally moved out of his room, one evening. He was exasperated with the lights on the streets, the noise of the vehicles and the people and the honks of the motor vehicles. He went to a bar where special service was provided. He could not bear the music in that bar. He ordered for a peg of Jack Daniels, neat. He looked around while taking the sips and his eyes stuck at someone. He ordered another one and kept his eyes on her moves. He ordered for a third and asked the waiter about her price. He did not negotiate and went to the room after her.

He stood while she undressed herself. He switched off the lights before she could stand completely naked in front of him.

"Why did you switch off the lights?" she asked.

"What's your name?"

"How does it matter?"

"It does. So, what's it?"

"Rakshita."

"How much would you charge for five days?"

"70K. And I won't understand why would you waste so much on me?"

"I will pay you 20K for five days."

"I am a business woman and it's a complete loss for me. You are good at negotiating but get into my shoes and satisfy me with a reason for such a negotiation. If you could satisfy me with your justification then I would accept your offer."

"Well, I always create win-win situation for everyone. Every business has its' down fall or a time when it's low. So you do have your time every month when you get no business. I will pay you for those times. I will be your only customer when you expect none or you can have no customers."

"Are you kidding me?"

"Does my voice seem so?"

"Why do you want me then?"

"That's not a matter of business for you. The ball is in your court and you have to decide the way you want to play. The goal post is clear and you have no obstruction. It's up to you whether you would like to hit it or miss it.", he paused and then continued, "I am leaving my number here. Get some clothes when you come because my dress won't fit you. Thank you.", he left her to ponder over their conversation.

He bought a bottle of Jack Daniels, a bottle of Johnnie Walker and a bottle of Dr. Pepper while returning. His phone buzzed.

"Hey, Ashi."

"Where were you? I was trying to reach you since long and there was no response. Do you have the slightest idea how tensed I was till this point?"

"Sorry, Ashi. I was out and did not realise the phone was ringing.", he said softly.

"I am glad that you finally went out after three months. Where had you been? Did you buy anything?"

"Yes, I bought three bottles of whiskey and scotch."

"What?"

"I realised that today is 9th."

"So what? I know that today is 9th of September."

"I did not know that it's September. I realised that it's 9ᵗʰ for which I want to celebrate this day with myself."

"Oh, okay. I remembered. I am sorry. I was so stressed as there was no response and that made me forget today's importance."

"You do not need to apologise. I understand. I am sorry for being the reason for your stress."

"It's alright, baba. Have fun and don't get completely immersed."

"I already am. Do take care."

It's the ninth of the month when they had confessed their emotions to each other for the very first time. It was again ninth of the month when she left him in the midst of the dunes where he saw nothing but sand and felt nothing but suffocation. Since the very day when she left him, he drank on the ninth and celebrated that day with himself. He spoke to her, read her messages, looked at her pictures and had candle light dinner with her, where he believed her to be sitting beside him as they always did when they had food together.

A few days passed when his phone buzzed, he received the call from an unknown number. He had not received anyone's call in the past couple of months apart from Afsheen's.

"Message me your address. I will be reaching in half an hour.", the voice said and disconnected the call before he could say anything.

After half an hour, he opened his door to see Rakshita at his doorstep.

He opened the door for her to come in. She was looking like heck of a beauty.

She entered to find apples, its' seeds or something related to it everywhere along with the empty bottles of scotch and whiskey.

"What the heck is this?", she exclaimed.

"If you don't like it then you surely can leave right away.", he said without any hesitation.

"I need someone to clean this mess."

"There is no one to clean this and I won't be asking anyone to clean this. As I said, you can leave if you don't like to stay here."

She did not say anything, kept her baggage in the corner of the room, took the broom and cleaned everything. She was about to open the bedroom when he stopped her.

"Don't ever open that door either in my presence or absence."

She did not say anything else.

"Do you have anything to eat? I am really hungry."

"I don't know. You can look in the kitchen or else you can order whatever you want to."

She went to kitchen to find nothing but apples in the refrigerator. She took one apple, washed it and ate it.

She ordered after scanning through a few menu cards which were lying around, he paid. She ate and he did not accompany her.

"Keep these 20K as we had decided. Thanks for showing up.", he said when she returned from the kitchen after cleaning the utensils.

"I will take it when I leave. You can give me then."

"You keep wherever you want to keep. Besides, don't speak to me much. Make yourself comfortable and do whatever you want to do apart from opening the bedroom."

She did not say him anything. She kept looking at him in the darkness. Whenever she needed light, she either went to the kitchen or to the restroom.

"I need 5000 bucks.", she demanded the following morning when he was lying on his mattress.

"It's there in the wallet on the dining table.", he said without opening his eyes.

"What if I take more without letting you know?"

"I don't have anything to lose anymore."

She took the amount from his wallet and left. She returned after two hours carrying groceries and vegetables.

"Would you please help me?", she requested.

He opened the door and didn't say anything, returned back to the couch and laid down.

From that evening, she cooked for both of them but he hardly ate.

"Don't force me to eat. You can force someone to keep the food in his mouth, but you never know whether he will gulp it or throw it. So it's better not to force anyone.", he said her once when she forced him to eat and irritated him by asking him again and again.

"You have lost enough in these couple of days or weeks. It seems as if you have stopped eating." She said remembering her first encounter with him.

"I am still alive. That's what matters."

"Do you love apples?"

"I have read in my childhood that 'an apple a day keeps the doctor away' so I eat two apples every day and that's enough to suffice my hunger. I eat when I am hungry, I don't eat because I have to or the time in the clock demands to eat."

She cooked and cleaned his room which was hers too for the time being. He never asked her to do so nor did she ever complain. He spoke to Afsheen on a daily basis. She wanted to make sure that he was alive. She knew that he would not be living his life but she would ensure that he was not dead. It was impossible for her to imaginee her life without him.

"Hey, Ashi. How are you?"

"I am good. How is my Dumbo doing?"

"I need you to help me which I have asked you earlier. It's time."

"Anything for you, dear."

"I want you to buy this flat and keep it as it is."

"What do you mean?"

"I mean I want you to buy this flat and maintain it the way it is now."

"Okay. It will be done. When do you want me to do it?"

"Whenever you feel like. I already had a word with the broker and he will take care of everything. I will message you his number."

"Is everything alright?"

"I don't understand this question. And you know what?"

"Say."

"If you can't live the way you have dreamt of, then you should at least die the way you have dreamt of."

"This time I want you to come with me. I don't want you to live alone. I don't want to lose you. I would love to take care of you and you are not turning me down like the last time. Do you understand?", she said firmly and he could feel her tears.

"Stop crying and I will come with you this time. But do buy this flat." He confirmed her.

———◆———

"Would you like to have dinner today?" she asked and he nodded.

She stayed with him like a partner of his. She took care of him, obeyed him, respected him, and listened to him like a wife. She had moved into his house like a girl who had just become a bride. There was no sign of her being a night-walker. She was just a girl rather a grown-up woman like any other human being. She was no more a business woman, but a friend to a friend, a sister to her brother, a mother to her children. No one could say about her profession any more. She was decent in her act and limited in her speech.

He switched on the lights. She served dinner for both of them and they both ate.

"No one will ever come here apart from Ashi.", he said her.

"Your girlfriend?"

"My best friend. If you do not find me some day when you get up and feel like leaving, you are free to do that. If you want to stay here till she comes, you can do that too and no one will ask you anything here. If you stay here till she comes, then you have to listen to her and do what she says."

"Okay."

"You are a good cook. I wish I would have tasted earlier."

"I have asked you many times to accompany me."

"Nothing happens before the right time. You came here when you felt. I wanted to go north and I am still waiting as the time has not come. It's so simple. Thank you, Hita."

"You are so matured. What's wrong with you?", she asked.

"I would like to know about you.", he stated, ignoring her question.

"I had always wanted to get into this profession."

"Explain."

"I lost my virginity with my boyfriend when I was in college. We had watched many porn movies together and that always excited me. I always wanted to be a painter as nature allures me. I always tried to paint her beauty. Every time it's different, her beauty is inexplicable. I never missed a chance to enjoy the serenity of her beauty. I stayed awake the whole night to capture her beauty. However the dream was not meant to be a reality for me. He left me because he got a rich whore and it took me a couple of days to gather myself. I could not focus on the nature, I could focus on nothing. I left those places which were haunting me so much. I came here and started my profession which had always excited me. I have no regrets. I am happy about the way it happened and whatever is happening. I meet different types of people every day that I collect many reasons to laugh. I meet people who cheat on their wives, who cheat on their girlfriends, who cheat on their children and parents. I meet people who were cheated by their wives or girlfriends. I meet people who are frustrated with everything that they need some spice in their life and go back to the frustration after getting the orgasm. I meet people who have no purpose in their life. Some people hurt me and I hurt some. Some people thank me for satisfying them and I wonder about my satisfaction. I wish someday someone will come and heal my bleeding, who will satisfy me mentally, and whom I will thank from the abyss of my heart. This is how my life is. And I love my life."

"Interesting."

"What about you?"

"Nothing."

"Why did you ask me to come to you?"

"I wanted you to."

"Why are you so indifferent?"

"Everyone is different."

"Have you always been like this?"

"It's the present which matters."

"Who is she?"

"An integral and indivisible part of my thoughts."

"Why are you doing this to yourself?"

"I can never do anything to anyone else."

"Why don't you live your life?"

"Everyone claims that they live their life. But how many actually do?"

"Point."

"Can I request you something?"

"Sure."

"I want you to leave this profession and do what most of the people do for their living. You are smart enough to crack any interview and you already have the experience of handling people. The choice is yours, after all."

"Don't think much about this girl."

"I don't have to. You have your life and you will live it the way you want. I would really appreciate if you change your profession."

"Why do you want that?"

"I seriously don't have an answer to this question. I don't know whether your profession is good or bad. I don't have any interest to know about it also. I just want you to change your profession. That's it."

"Thank you for being so nice to me. And, thank you."

"Thank yourself for whatever you have."

"Can I ask you something?"

"Sure. And yes, the food was delicious. Thank you for such a wonderful evening and a yummy dinner."

"Can I stay with you like this forever?"

He laughed at this question.

"I fell in love with you and I just want to be with you forever. I have no expectations from you, I just want to be with you."

He could not control his laugh.

———✧———

The following morning when she woke up, she did not find him and Afsheen arrived in the late afternoon.

Rakshita opened the door with a hope that he had returned and saw Afsheen in front of her. Afsheen was shocked to see Rakshita as he had never mentioned her during their conversation.

"Who are you?"

"I am Rakshita and you are Ashi. Right?"

"Right and where is he?"

"I don't know. I thought it's him."

"I need you to explain everything."

"I am a business woman whom he has paid to be here for five days and I am here since a couple of weeks, I believe, without asking him anything extra and leaving my profession. I wanted to penetrate him as he left me with millions of questions from the very first day we met. He is such a thick skin that he never let me touch him, forget about penetrating his mind or heart. He told me yesterday that you will come some day and I did not know that you will come so soon. Last night he had dinner for the first time in last few weeks. I did not see him eating, he just kept boozing and locking himself in the bedroom for hours. He did not even speak to me much. He sometimes played the same song for hours which irritated me and he used his headphone when I told him about this. He received no one's calls but yours. He is in love, he deeply loves someone. I wanted to take care of him just because of the way he is. I have never seen such a man throughout my life. He is different, completely different from everyone I have ever seen."

"What's there in the bedroom?"

"I don't know. He asked me not to open it and I never did."

She opened the door and her mouth fell apart when she saw the photos of Sayuri everywhere in the room. Everything was maintained properly and it was impossible to find even a particle of dust. The room seemed like a place of sanctity to her. It was heavenly and all the positive energy flowed to her when they entered. There was a bunch of paper lying on the bed and a letter above it.

"Dear Ashi,

If you are reading this letter, it means I am long gone. I wished I could stay with you but I was unable to control my mind. It has been almost six months that I had not spoken to her or seen her and I have been thinking about her more and more with every passing moment. I am missing her more than the last moment. It's getting impossible for me to live without her. I am unable to survive even. I could not breathe, I could not laugh, I could not cry. I am no more what I was, I had always thought of living a life but it's been impossible for me to do so.

She had wanted me to write and this is what I have written in these months. Get the print and give it to her. This copy is all yours. You do whatever you want to do with it.

I am sorry for leaving you. I really did not want that but I am helpless. I can't live like a hypocrite. I would expect your forgiveness. You are hell of a friend and I will pray to God whom you believe so much to keep you safe in His hands. You don't need to miss me as you have always done. Do take care of yourself as you would have done if I would have been around. Never forget that I have always respected you two and never let that be buried like emotions are buried these days in a couple of weeks.

I love you and Saaya is my soul."

Afsheen had never seen Sayuri before and she realised how beautiful she must have been and then looked at Rakshita to understand that she had a great resemblance with Sayuri for which he was with her. Rakshita was surprised to see herself in the photos initially and then realised that it's someone else's after giving a close look at the photos.

"Rakshita, I am really thankful to you for taking care of him for a few weeks. Did he tell you about his departure?"

"No, but he might have gone north as he mentioned to me about it last night over dinner."

"Thank you. I want you to leave now. How much do I have to pay you?"

"You don't have to buy emotions, Madam. No one can ever pay for love, the divine, the unconditional love."

"Don't love him or else you will ruin your life."

"I made my life, not ruined, by knowing what love is and thanks to him. And for your information, for the first time I was slapped for undressing a man or a guy and to my surprise, he was a virgin."

"You should better leave now and thank you."

Rakshita left without saying anything and Afsheen cried holding his memories close to her heart.

<hr>

"Hi, Sayuri."

"Who is this?"

"I want to meet you now. Where are you?"

"Who are you?"

"Are you in office?"

"Yes, but who are you? Would you please reply to my question?"

"I will introduce myself in half an hour. You are leaving office then. You have only half an hour to wrap up your work."

And the call was dropped before she could say something.

"I would like to meet Sayuri." Afsheen told the receptionist.

"Do you have an appointment?"

"Yes, I do.".

"Please sit and I will inform her."

Sayuri came out to see her visitor.

"Hi, it's Afsheen."

"Hello.", she said with a shock in her eyes.

"I would like you to leave office now rather than saying me how stuck you are with your work and without letting me create a scene. Please."

"Give me ten minutes."

"All yours."

She returned in fifteen minutes and they went to the nearby cafeteria.

"I never wanted to meet you but I had to. That's what fate has decided."

"You speak like him."

"He does not speak like this anymore and for your information, he hardly speaks these days."

"Why did you want to meet me?"

"I have no allegations. He would have never preferred me accusing someone for something. He always preferred to accuse himself whenever something went wrong. I am happy to hear that you are getting married. Congratulations."

"Thank you but you did not want to meet me just to congratulate."

"You sacrificed your love for your parents and he is sacrificing his life for his love. I want my friend back. You have everyone in your life. He never had anyone apart from us and I never had anyone apart from him. Do you understand what I am talking about?"

She was speechless. She nodded and remained mum.

"I don't know what your relationship was and what happened between you two, I just know that I don't want to be the victim. I know that he was unpredictable, no one knew how would he react to what but he was great at his heart. He never remembered anything about anyone but he could look into someone's eyes for a moment and could say his state of emotion and could get him back to his life. He would just listen to someone's "hello' over the phone and he could say the phase she/he was going through. He never respected anyone apart from us, his life was engulfed with us. I tried to get him back from all these, the more I tried the more he got into you. He was damn addicted to you. I have seen people getting addicted to alcohol, drugs and smoking but he got addicted to you. I have never seen anyone getting addicted to another human being. He thought that time will heal him but alas. You know what?"

"Hmm?', Sayuri responded unconsciously.

"He had told me that he always loved the way you say 'hmm'. Anyway, he might have told you that he had many girls in his life but I can assure you that he never had anyone in his life. The perception of the people only created this. If you spend some more time with a girl and say her that you love her then that's an affair and if you do the same with a guy then it's friendship. That's disgusting. You believe or you don't, but the reality is, he had never been in love with any of them or else he would not have left anyone. I have seen girls falling for him during the school and college days but he never cared about anyone. Girls have affair with others and if they were asked how they expect a guy to be like, then their answer went for him. He was not handsome, he was neither that great looking nor did he have a good height but he was different in his own way. He is the perfect guy for any girl if she could simply take care of his incalculable mood.

I have been with him since ages. He never cared to touch me even once. I love him, Sayuri and being a girl I know that you had sensed it and you must have felt jealous of me but he never thought of ripping me off. He cared for me and he was always there with me but he never thought of deflowering me. I would have easily done that with him if he would have asked once or I would have ever felt some sign from him. He never took advantage of me or my parents or anything. My father had told me once that he would be completely lost if he ever loses his love and I would be the luckiest girl if he could ever fall in love with me. He had warned me not to fall in love with him. But alas!!!! He never fell in love with me and I devoted myself to him. Anyways. Sayuri, I just want you to get him his life back."

"I won't speak to him."

"I hope his death will complete your sacrifice. I don't have anything else to say then."

Afsheen took out the packet which she had brought along with her and handed over to Sayuri.

"What's this?", she asked while her tears rolled down her cheeks.

"This is what he had done in last six months and this is what you have asked him to do."

She opened the packet to see the book which he had written. She turned the pages when Afsheen gave her another wrapped item. She took it from her and opened the wrap to see the platinum ring which engraved "Saaya" on it.

"This is what he wanted to give you as you had wished for it and it was his dream to give you. He had always wanted to fulfil all your dreams."

Her phone buzzed. She received an image from the guy whom she had asked to track him in north.

"Congratulations, Sayuri.", she told her while holding her tears back and carrying a sarcastic silent smile on her face. She forwarded that image to her.

She opened the image to understand the expression of Afsheen and became expressionless.

There was a guy lying on the nature's lap completely covered with snow as if the nature had covered him with the white blanket to bestow upon her love for the guy who had loved her a lot and whose soul had released his body.

Ashi drank the Cappuccino which she had ordered and Saaya kept gazing at the photo while tears rolled down her eyes.

The book was lying on the table with its' last page and the last sentence said

"Love is inevitable and so is death; love is eternal and so is soul."